# The War To E
# Chains

by

## Tessa Shutter

*Tessa Shutter*

ISBN: 9798594833883

PUBLISH**NATION**
www.publishnation.co.uk

*To my sisters and brother, for helping me with the front cover.*
*To my parents, my unofficial editors.*
*To my friends, who believed in my writing from day one.*

# Prologue

My land is battle scarred, disfigured to the bone, and my heart is scared along with it. At least there's peace now, I almost smile at the irony, almost. Why does the thing I've wanted for nearly three years now leave me with such distaste and horror? Because of what comes with it, nothing good can happen without a consequence.

Like how a princess does not wear a crown without a death, like how a war is not won without losses, like how there is never freedom without bondage. My life is not one to be enjoyed now, forget my title, forget my kingdom, and look into my heart. See the love that has been wrenched from it, see the wounds that lattice it, see the ice that strengthens it. You do not really know someone without walking in their shoes, please if you are still affirmed that I am the luckiest person on earth be my guest, come now and see the last few years walking in my shoes.

# A Presence in Court

"Princess, your father requests your presence in court today." I sighed and looked up at Deon, my bodyguard. Well I say "bodyguard;" more like companion and friend. Deon's alright I suppose, better than Hako's bodyguard anyhow. Deon's a Centaur with a magnificent body of shining black sleek fur. Deon's chest was covered by one of the black, clean cut, cloth shirts the human guards were wearing. My father does not think it's fit for me to spend so much time with a handsome bare-chested centaur. It's as if he doesn't trust me, to think of it. Next to Deon was Melissa, my handmaid. She was a small wood elf, older than me, twenty-seven, I think. Melissa walked into my chambers and took a simple white dress out of my wardrobe. It was chased with a thin line of gold, marking me out as part of the royal family. I stood up from my desk where I was writing and, with a glance to make sure Deon had closed the door and was taking his post outside, slipped off my tunic.

After Melissa had drawn me a bath and I'd washed, I put on the dress and Melissa started to do my hair, deftly braiding two thin plaits at the front of my head, she pulled them back keeping my flowing long locks out of my face. Once I was done, Melissa smiled and called to Deon,
"Deon! She's ready." Deon opened the door and outstretched his hand. With a reluctant sigh I took it and let myself be hoisted onto his back.

Deon walked slowly through the palace. We call it our castle, but it is not. It's not like the decrepit old things that they have in some other kingdoms. Ours is more disbanded little huts which make up every chamber, connected by thick wooden walkways. The huts are stunningly beautiful, organic and wooden, flowing into one another in such a majestically fluid way. The stone walls are full of climbing flowers and beds of grasses fringing the edges. We're surrounded by a tall, but easy to get through wall, there are huge over the top gates that always have at least six guards. There are watch towers too. The castle sits on the peak of a large hill and from it you can see all down to the valley and everything in perfect detail as we aren't too high but just high enough for an entire overview. Once we passed the gates, I slipped off Deon's back.

"Where's Storm?" I asked, referring to my horse. Deon pointed to the approaching figure of an elven stable boy holding Storm gingerly. Storm did not look impressed by the boy and tossed his head, huffing at me.

"Your horse my lady," he said with a smile. I looked more closely at the boy.

"Are you new here?" I asked. He was about my age, maybe a little older, with long feathery brown hair and amber eyes. The boy nodded.

"Y-yeah, I started yesterday, just helping out a little, you know. I'm in training for the army. My father - he was a general. General Yan, but um… he died, a few months ago. As is customary for the children of guards and soldiers, I was taken in by the palace. I help as a groom at the stables in my spare time. Good to keep busy, you know." I smiled, and the boy's eyes were saddened and mournful but, in a heart, meltingly warm way.

"I'm so sorry. I hope you can find a place in the army and a family with somebody." I said. It was a mainstream answer, when giving somebody condolences, to just wish them a new family and a place in their job. It was easy, but the boy seemed to think more of it. He beamed at me and bowed slightly.

"Thank you, my lady. I hope your horse has been sufficiently cared for and groomed." I nodded, taking Storm's reins.

"I'm sure he will have been. Sorry, what's your name?" The boy smiled.

"Asir, please call me Asir." I smiled and turned away,

"Well I hope to see you again sometime, Asir." Asir nodded, grinning,

"I'd like that, Princess."

"Nice boy," Deon noted as we trotted down the hill into the forest at the base.

"Yeah, I guess. I just feel so sorry for him," I replied. Deon shrugged.

"His case isn't so unusual."

"Yes, but usually when that's happened the elves just seem so broken, but he seems strong and…" Deon interrupted me with a knowing shake of the head.

"Oh no, princess, not again, don't go getting starry eyed about another dashing youth with sad eyes." I laughed.

"You make it sound like it happens all the time." Deon shrugged and began counting on his fingers.

"First there was that merboy with the injured tail, because he was stupid enough to swim in that unstable cave."

"He thought his sister might be stuck in there!" I protested, but Deon continued,

"Then that valiant little wood elf with the baby sister." I shouted out my annoyance at this one.

"She had to support a five-year-old girl with absolutely no parental guidance." Deon nodded dismissively and went on.

3

"Then you had those two juvenile centaurs, first the blonde one then, once he ended it, that other one with the dark hair."

"They were both very sweet and courageous boys," I added. Deon shrugged.

"Then that mermaid," I smiled,

"Amaryllis was so gracious and kind," Deon didn't seem to acknowledge my comment.

"And who could forget the last elf you were with? Tobias was it or Tibius?" I rolled my eyes,

"Tiberis, his name was Tiberis." Deon shrugged again,

"I think my point is proven. Anyway, the longest of those relationships only lasted about two months. There's no point in becoming involved with anyone because you'll only end up hurt." I smiled and pulled Storm to a halt.

"I appreciate that you don't want me to get hurt but I can survive a little hurt if it means I can have a month or two of happiness." Deon shrugged again,

"I'm here to save your life, not your heart, princess. I can't stop you."

When we reached the forest and waited outside the glade where my father would be holding his council, I dismounted from Storm and readily allowed a wood elf to place a circlet of silver upon my head. Then as I turned to the passageway of bent together willow branches, Deon cried out in a loud carrying voice.

"Please all be silent and respectful for the heir to the elven throne of Charyass, Princess Athena."

I walked through, easily, Deon trotting behind me. I inclined my head to the surrounding advisors and generals of my father. The council were all seated on living thrones made from the trees and bushes themselves and twisted into a seating shape. Then I reached my father, sitting in his great throne of stone, engraved with elvish runes and writings, crested in some places with moss and set a few meters in front of the sacred pool. Behind the pool a craggy rock face was marked by a trickling waterfall feeding the shining blue waters. My father looked at me, his eyes glistened with love and his face creased with a smile. The king's long beard and hair were a dark blonde colour. His ears were long and sharply pointed. My throne was near my father's; it was a spherical cocoon made of a bush of fine bending willowy branches that in the summer were festooned by miniature white and pink flowers. I quickly took my seat and Deon stood beside me. My father raised his voice and spoke.

"Now we are all present I would like to begin by addressing the request Macos was asking of me."

General Macos was the General in the army who trained all the initial recruits before they separated into specific skill sets. Macos stood up and bowed to the king,

"With regard to our newest recruit sir, a certain Asir I request that he should be withdrawn from the army." A shocked silence was left among the court. The elven army is for all to join no matter species, gender or anything. Pass the first physical and mental test and you're in. Only a gross misdemeanor will warrant your removal. Father stared at Macos.

"What could possibly promote these feelings after only a day's work?" Macos smiled.

"I am coming to that, my king, and I have several points to put forward. The boy is… wayward. Last night he was talking to some friends when he began speaking ill of one of his superiors, stating that he could arch better than them and wondering how they got into the army. This is blatant arrogance." The king frowned,

5

"Macos I hope you can realize that this is common among the new recruits they don't yet know the way of things." Macos was about to sit down when a young elven boy ran into the glade and whispered something in his ear. Macos beamed cruelly and said.

"You will find this far worse my king. Today Asir was flirting with the princess."

All eyes turned to me, they weren't surprised - more annoyed, especially my father's gaze. They all seemed to say, "Oh she's at it again. All right then." I glared defiantly at Macos waiting for him to say his piece.

"When Asir brought the princess her horse she asked him if he was new. To this yes/no question, Asir's reply was his entire life story." Macos paused to let it sink in then continued. "The Princess offered her condolences and then Asir said he hoped the horse had been well groomed, the princess replied he had been and then asked his name." The Court grunted in surprise, Macos continued his eyes glinting,

"The princess said she'd like to see him again and Asir replied and I quote," Macos looked down at a piece of paper than the boy had given to him, "I'd like that princess." Macos sat down and the king looked at me.

"Athena," Father said, his voice slightly strangled. "Is this true?" I shook my head.

"No, father. It is not. We had a nice conversation and I liked him. Is having friends a crime? I said I would like to have another conversation and he agreed. I see nothing wrong. Asir is a good elf and he should remain in the army, that is what I say." Father nodded, he looked at Macos and said,

"Apologies Macos, but it seems your little friend misunderstood the meaning of the conversation, it seems

6

that it was innocent; at least fairly innocent." Father gave me a look that read, "Talk later."

After a while longer the king said the meeting of the day was over. I was about to leave along with the others but as I had feared he signaled me to wait. Once everyone had left, I went over to stand by his throne.

"Were you flirting with this boy?" Father asked, his voice stern. I shrugged.

"'Flirting' is a strong word. If you were asking if I was attracted to him, then yes. Yes, I was attracted, but flirting is a strong word. My words may have been leaning towards the suggestive, but I wouldn't say I was flirting per se." My father rested his head in hands,

"Not another one Athena!"

I frowned. "Look. You liked Tiberis. If he hadn't changed, you would have been happy with me marrying him." Father nodded and sighed,

"Tiberis was in my interests, good boy, under the radar, relatively high birth, not standing to lead you to any kind of disgrace, If you were going to marry someone it would have to be someone like Tiberis, who, by the way, is still loving and available." I glared at my father,

"Who cares," was my reply. Father took my hand and looked into my eyes with a hard and solid gaze.

"Your father cares, Athena. As does the king. A boy whom Macos is pushing to have out of the army is in no way, shape or form a proper suitor for the heir to the throne. Now if you were interested in Macos's son..." I snorted at that.

"Levi is a bore, and he's horrible to me. Anyway, isn't it Hako you're meant to be worried about marrying off? I'm going to rule the kingdom, no matter what." Father nodded.

"I know you are, but I'd hate for you to rule it with the wrong person by your side."

7

Deon took me back to the palace and I went straight to my room. Standing up there at the highest pinnacle you could see everything in the valley below. In the water of a winding river, frolicked merpeople, scales shining azure blue and emerald green, fins flicking up the water high, the droplets being lit by the sun to shine in a mesmerizing rainbow. At the river's edge stood the elegant bodies of deer. The tentative and ungainly steps of a fawn brought a brief smile to my lips. Hidden, also in the tall grass, was a manticore pup, small and slightly cute without a mane nor properly developed wings yet. I watched as it playfully pretended to stalk the deer, toying with the idea of hunting. The forests were always beautiful. Wood elves skipped in and out, dancing along the forest edge. Children with bright laughing eyes and intricately plaited and braided hair, were wreathed in eye catching smiles. Suddenly the valley went quiet. A dark shadow passed overhead, eclipsing almost the entire meadow. I looked up. The dragon was a deep burgundy, it's huge leathery wings only occasionally giving a lazy flap. It was a magnificent creature. A male, fully grown; beautiful in a way majestic. It soon passed and light returned to the valley. The air hummed with joyous energy; you could see and hear the peace of it all. You just wanted to jump into it. A Griffin flapped overhead; far smaller than the dragon, no bigger than the average horse, the huge coppery brown feathered wings flapping and the sun highlighting the streaks of gold at the creature's head. Its hind quarters were all lion, sleek and fast, strong and powerful. Its fast eyes pinpointed the fawn and it swooped down, the deer scattered, but the fawn wasn't fast enough. In moments it had been killed with a slash to the heart and then carried away in the Griffin's claws. The Griffin flapped back towards its mountain home, the lion's tail twitching. A centaur galloped out of the wood, tall and strong, the

8

chest bristling with muscle, the long brown hair streaming out in the wind. It was a young one, in its twenties or so. But Centaurs live twice as long as Elves. After him came a much younger centaur, around my age, maybe a little older I guessed. They looked similar though the younger one had far darker hair, almost black. Brothers, I guessed. They each had a bow and quiver strapped to their backs, so I guessed they were out hunting. A wood elf girl stepped towards the younger one, she was about his age, maybe a little older. She smiled flirtatiously and flicked a braid of hair. They seemed to be acquainted, a couple I guessed. She stroked his flank and then he lifted her up into a kiss. Inter species relationships only work if you swear to not have children. An elf giving birth to a centaur would not be a pretty sight. The elder brother seemed bored by his sibling's show of affection. He casually shot a hare and handed the dead corpse to one of the gawking wood elf girls. Elven girls think Centaurs are amazing; they're mad about them. I expect it's the galloping thing. I act like I am superior but as Deon mentioned I've had my fair share of centaur boys. I can testify they are stunning. Also, the whole, "Jump on my back, let's go for a ride," is pretty alluring in some ways. Oh, the days I spent on Nix's back… Anyway, the Centaurs in the valley were being watched by the male wood elves with a sure envy and annoyance but also a slight note of admiration. Suddenly the young one hugged his she-elf friend goodbye and turned to his brother who began galloping off once again. For a moment everything was normal. Then you smelt it. A mix of the rotting smell of Sulphur and the sharp throat catching stench of acidic poison, it was the scent of a Manticore.

The elves hurried back into the woods; mothers and fathers hurrying their children further into the forest. The merpeople plunged deep into the depths out of sight, activating their gills so they could breathe. The herd of deer which had reformed after the Griffin had departed, scattered once again to be away from this danger, everyone could sense and smell it. Then it arrived, the immense form of the Manticore, larger than any horse, huge with a roaring head covered in the long flowing lion's mane that marked it out as a male. Its eyes were red and eerie; the maw dripping with green toxic saliva, and full of ferocious fangs. The mane was a rich burgundy red in colour; the colour of dark fire. The fur and body were golden and sleek, soft and beautiful. But the huge dragon wings protruding from the shoulders were spread wide, menacingly high. The scorpion's tail dangled, the tip hovering just between the animal's shoulder blades. It glowed with green venom. The creature's eyes were searching, scanning the valley and sniffing for the scent of its cub. A mewling cry from the cub giving away its place. The Manticore leapt forward, landing on it and catching the animal up in its mouth. This is what happens when a cub wanders too far from the den, it's mother, or father comes to find it and they will not stop for anything between them and their child. Manticores are good parents, I always thought. The Manticore turned and stalked away, holding its cub. Bit by bit the creatures came out again; first the merpeople, peeping above the waterline cautiously, then leaping up onto the surface again; then the elven children looking rattled and shaken but eyes and faces glowing with adrenalin. I bet their parents didn't care who they married, I bet their parents didn't care if they were flirting or not, I bet they didn't have horrible people pushing to objectify them. I bet... I brought my rants to a halt. It wouldn't do; I had far more responsibility and it wasn't my fault I'd been born a high elf. I was a high elf, meaning I'm a member of the royal family. So, I have to stay in my place; if I ever wanted to rule that is.

There was a gentle knock on the door.

"Come in." I called. I knew it was Hako. He always knocks gently. He's scared of me you see, and quite rightly too. Hako walked in smiling. Hako's two years younger than me, so sixteen. Tall and muscular, yet leaner than a lot of elves with a rangier body suited for speed. He has my blue eyes and blonde hair, but his skin is a shade or two darker than my own, rich brown, whereas mine is more mahogany. Hako was wearing a short cream-colored training tunic and his bow and quiver were on his back. I guess he must have just come from training. I train too but, on the days, when Father wants me to hold presence in court I'm unable to.

"So how was it today?" Hako asked, sitting down on one of the chairs by my bed.

"Good, but Macos caught me flirting with the new stable groom."

Hako gave a low whistle. "The king wasn't happy?"

"Not at all. I like him though; he's called Asir."

Hako raised his eyes upwards. "Honestly, Athena, again?!"

I pushed him playfully. "Why does everyone act like I'm some serial lover?"

Hako shrugged. "You're not. just... six, in one year for the high elven princess and heir to the throne."

I rolled my eyes.

"Yes, yes, they love to prey on it. The desirable elven princess likes to play the field. I am fully aware of why everyone makes such a big deal about it."

Hako smiled.

"Well if you like Asir, go on ahead. Is he the one with the long hair and the eyes?"

I frowned. "How did you know?"

Hako laughed. "He is SOOO your type."

I looked at Hako indignantly. "My type?"

Hako nodded. "Long hair, tall, lean, warm eyes that you can just sink deep into and *get lost inside their liquid amber pools*." I swatted him at the romantic poet persona he took on when describing the eyes.

"So, what if I have a type, I know what I like." I said defiantly.

Hako shrugged, holding his hands up.

"And it's not like you don't."

Hako's eyes widened.

"Tell me more." I yawned and sighed. "Well you're so desperate anything vaguely humanoid."

Hako frowned. "Yeah pretty much, but I'm not too mad for blondes." I raised my eyebrows.

"Since when?"

Hako smiled. "Since I had to spend my life with the worst one ever!"

I pulled him off the chair, tackling him onto my bed, the two of us rolled around together for a while, joined in playful spirit and kinship, laughing and tussling together. Happy and free, for a brief few minutes. No longer burdened by any such responsibilities as power or pressure; just two teenagers having some fun.

# The Newcomer

The next morning, I was surprised to find that Deon was at the door with Melissa once again requesting my presence in court.

"But I went yesterday." I moaned as Melissa braided my hair.

"There is a newcomer requesting an audience with the king." Melissa said as she deftly pulled my two thin plaits away and secured them with a thin hair band. I felt surprised even more so when instead of my usual white dress a more ceremonial ornate one was laid out for me, I dutifully put it on and left my chambers astride Deon's back.

Storm was saddled and bridled in his ceremonial tack as well, embroidered with the Elven crest. Asir brought him to me. He looked more handsome today, more at ease and put together. While Deon was looking away Asir pulled me close to him and whispered:

"I'm sorry about what the general said earlier. I didn't mean to flirt, and now your father is aware it's best I stay away from you. I can get another groom to bring the horses."

I laughed and shook my head.

"Not on your life. I have power over every one of those sappy generals and I tell you when you should stop bringing my horses to me."

Asir smiled sheepishly. "Yeah, yeah of course, thank you."

I grinned.

"No problem.   Also," I smiled at Storm admiring his finely braided mane, knotted up properly to leave his muscular and gleaming dark neck exposed.

13

"Storm's never had a better groom."

I reached the court as usual, but the wood elves that served me seemed flustered, furtive, maybe even scared. I hurried into the clearing. I wasn't exactly nailing the elegant glide I had been taught but it was close enough. The guest was not yet here I noted, and I gently curtseyed to my father before taking my seat. We all watched and waited for a while. Then a voice announced.
"Please show respect for Casseil of Barrow."

The man entered or rather his mount did. A Griffin; huge and powerful, stalking forward; its feathers ruffled and mangy; its eyes were wild and pained. And it only took a glance to see why. A bridle similar to that of a horse was around the creature's head, an ugly bit jammed tightly between its beak. A hard saddle was upon its back and sitting on it gripping the reins that connected the cruel bridle to it was a human. We knew of humans of course, we even had a few at the palace, outcasts from their own kingdoms; come to Charyass for a better life. But we had never seen one so spectacular as this. They were generally thin and weary from the journey but this man was huge. Muscles pushed at his battle armour; a sword at his hip and a shield strapped to his back. He was taller and broader than my father, a Herculean giant in some ways; huge and fearsome, tall and powerful. His skin was dark, and his head was entirely shaven. On his boots were sharp spurs, no doubt to kick the Griffin and make it run. Casseil's face bore the shadow of a beard and his eyes gleamed coal black out of his face. Casseil swung leisurely off his Griffin and walked towards the king. I immediately hated him. There is a test I mentally do with male newcomers. It's not hard if they look at me, as well as all the others and at least incline their head or even better bow, then the jury is still out. But

14

if they don't look, I don't like them and Casseil acted as if I wasn't there.

"What is the meaning of this?" Father asked, clicking his fingers at a waiting wood elf. "Get that… thing off that poor animal before it goes completely crazy." Cassiel held up his hands in protest, when he spoke his voice was smooth, his words honey sweet and persuasive.

"Oh sir, please no. The Griffin is being completely fine, honestly, completely fine." He spoke Elfish badly, haltingly with a strong accent of some kind. Father glared at the Griffin. "He doesn't look fine to me."

Cassiel nodded. "I understand how this situation might er… come across but this is the new way of things where I come from. We harness these creatures and make them work for us. We can do everything and anything, all with just the tug of a chain or prod of a hot iron." Rage filled me.

"What is this, the enslaving of the creatures that created us, the most ancient beings alive, the things that were here long before and will no doubt be here long after all of us." I shouted, leaping up. Cassiel finally looked at me but with the superior look of someone who thinks I'm just a silly child.

"Please, king, control your daughter."

For a dangerous moment I thought Father would agree but instead he stood too, his eyes ablaze like twin balls of blue fire.

"My daughter needs no controlling! On the contrary I am in wholehearted agreement and she is Princess Athena to you, heir to the throne." Casseil didn't show any humbleness under the gaze of my father, he simply gave me a cool look.

"So, the woman can lead here too then, I suppose one of the many reasons it's such a mess."

The court murmured and shifted in anger. all eyes were on Casseil and all eyes were hating him. Father sat back down, forcing a smile.

"What have you come to discuss, Casseil? You will understand you aren't painting yourself in the best light here." Casseil shrugged.

"I have come to make a proposition: You adopt our practices, harness the animals, rein in the dragons and Griffins so to speak, ride the Manticores. We have an army, a huge one, full of Centaurs and Elves, Merpeople and Griffins. We even have three Dragons. We are on our way to having the world under us and at our fingertips. We conquer all in our wake, but......" Casseil let silence fall for a moment then continued.

"If you were to ally with us, we could leave your kingdom out of it and bypass you, if you gave us the right of passage through of course." The king steepled his fingers and looked down at Casseil.

"This army of yours, the centaurs, the elves, the merpeople, did they join of their own free will?" Casseil laughed. "Why of course not. We captured them, naturally."

Father nodded.

"Alright, be on your way Casseil, we refuse your proposition."

The onlookers sighed in relief and for a moment all tension was gone, until the look on Casseil's face was apparent.

"You don't know what you're doing. We will crush you in days. You will be nothing without the creatures controlled and harnessed. Why don't you capture them? You are stronger, you are smarter, you are better, you are more powerful. One last chance."

Father smiled slightly. His sky-blue eyes coolly watching Cassiel.

"Tell me, does that Griffin look free to you?"

Casseil shook his head with a snort. "Why of course not, he is mine."

Father gave a cold scathing look and continued.

"And yet they are supposed to be wilder than our dreams, stronger than our chains and more joyful than our children."

Casseil laughed "You do the same with horses."

The king laughed too but not as if he found it funny like he was amused at Casseil's stupidity.

"Horses - they are able to bond with you. A horse can be a friend but not on equal terms. A horse can love and worship, same with a dog, but a Dragon, a Griffin, a Phoenix? They are different; they are animals that take pride in their independence; their ruthless ferocity; their wild tendencies. If they dare to love a human, they love as equal friends, and they don't love for long, they don't give second chances, they don't give you leeway, they will love until they hate, one second of hate and they are gone." I stared at Father. he spoke like he was remembering something half forgotten, something painful. The King pointed at the Griffin whose eyes were burning, and whose mouth was foaming from the hard bit. "You look into that Beast's eyes and tell me you see any love."

Casseil glared at the king. He was angry, incredibly angry,

"You can recite all the worthless poetry you care for but we know what we're doing. This beast has no soul. It is nothing. It is worthless. We... we have the power and we are going to use it." Casseil leapt upon his Griffin yanking at the reins so it reared up high, then he pointed a finger straight at Father. "Make ready. Make ready your armies

17

and make ready your weapons because you are going to war. Then make ready your funeral pyres and make ready your clothes of mourning because many will lose their lives. Then, make ready your families and make ready your homes because you are going to lose your kingdom. And finally, make ready your minds and make ready your bodies because then you will lose your liberty."

Casseil rode away leaving a shocked and scared silence.

Finally, Macos spoke. "The new recruits can survive in the line of fire, a lot of natural talent, nothing like hands on experience." Another general stated that the Centaur and Merpeople recruits were also capable. Someone else monologued about how ready we were, but Father said nothing. After more silence he finally said.

"We need the beasts." Uproar exuded. I streaked over to Father.

"You mean join them? How could you say that?" I screamed. Around us Generals and advisors began to fight together shouting to each other. Father rubbed his face wearily then called out.

"No! Let a king finish his sentence." There was silence again. "Right, as I was saying, we need to get the creatures to fight with us, not for us, we can persuade most of them, it's just the Dragons I'm worried about." I nodded.

"I'll go. I'll go into Griffin mountain to see if I can get them on board. On Storm it should only take a day or so." Father agreed to my offer, thanking me greatly.

"I'll set up other expeditions, we shall not ask the dragons until absolutely necessary; no use risking good soldiers." Father paused then suddenly he had his battle face on. He looked deadly serious.

"I'll need scouts all over. See how long till they get there. Tell the blacksmiths we're going to need a lot of armour and weapons for the new recruits. Get to your regiments all of you. Everyone spread the word. We are going to war. we need to beat them, not just for Charyass, for all the kingdoms that lie beyond."

I sat on my bed, thinking. The day Cassiel had come had been hectic. I'd been trained relentlessly and then given a crash course in leadership before being assigned a small group of elite recruits, only about two hundred, but still a lot since I'd never led any proper armies. Today I was about to ride over to Mount Griffin to recruit the Griffins. Deon would accompany me, and I didn't really mind. The trip would take a few days and getting lost alone up there would be truly awful. A knock on my door signaled Deon's entry. He came with Melissa on his back holding my armour. The elven armour is light and easy to move in, with arm and leg guards of black iron held on with hard leather. There's a breastplate with a tree embossed upon it in emerald. Melissa immediately went to my hair, of course, and Deon who was holding two fur cloaks. I assumed one was for me one for him. He tossed me mine. It was a deep green and looked warm and cozy, beautifully lined and hooded. Melissa did my hair in two long plaits for battle falling evenly down my back. They clung to my scalp starting early just where my hairline begins rising on top of the hair. Then I put on thick underclothes before having my amor strapped onto me bit by bit. Finally, my weapons were clipped on, my bow and quiver attached to the back of my battle harness and my dual daggers at each hip. Deon handed me my cloak and I put it on over my armour.

"You look just like your mother." I turned to see Father standing in the doorway.

"Oh, ugh hey." I said. Father rarely came to see me get ready. He likes to see the finished product. When I was little, I would moan about it to my handmaids. Sometimes Mother used to braid my hair instead of a handmaid and I

19

always wished that Father would as well. Mother would always say he was busy running the kingdom and all she had to do was look after the children. It was a joke of course. Mother did an awful lot, but she always found time to come and see me getting ready.

Father walked in and kissed me on the head. "Hako's jealous, you know, poor boy."

I laughed.

Father and Hako were close in a way but Hako was very eager to please. He worshipped Father. I tolerated him. "Remember to say goodbye. He's worried about you." Father added. I smiled.

"I'll be fine. It'll take three days maximum, and we'll hopefully be back with a troop of happy Griffins ready for combat."

Father smiled. "I'm sending ten men for the Manticores, but just my little girl for the Griffins."

I grinned and gave him a little swift hug.

"Well luckily for you, your little girl is far stronger than ten men."

Storm was saddled and ready when I arrived outside the gates. A nervous Asir was holding him.

"Shouldn't you be training and everything." I said, once I'd mounted Storm.

Asir shrugged. "I had some free time and wanted to see you off. I-I hope you get them on board. My friend - he's a scout, says this is a hard army, a really big army and we're going to be hard pressed to beat them, but we will, I'm sure of it." I smiled.

"Thanks, Asir. I hope if it does anything good this war will bring us closer together. I checked you're in my regiment, so get ready to answer to me."

Asir smiled. "Like I didn't already know my lady."

20

I laughed and shrugged then clicked my tongue at Storm and started. I called a goodbye back behind me to the palace and with Deon cantering at my side, I was off.

# Griffin Mountain

We travelled the entire day, moving through forests and meadows, savannahs and valleys. Charyass is a very varied kingdom. The terrain changes so fluidly we even ended up along the seafront. The mer people of the sea are a different species to the freshwater merpeople. They are in a word. Saltier. More vicious and mischievous, with more of a tendency for wild partying and don't get me started on their love lives and drama. We made camp on the cliff edge. I unsaddled Storm and let him graze. Deon started a fire and I dug around in the saddle bags for our food. We dined on dried beef jerky and some foraged mushrooms. I rolled up in my cloak and lay on my back gazing at the stars. Deon removed his cloak and, in a way, customary of Centaurs draped it over his horse body. I looked at the clear and bright stars. When I was eleven, a year after my mother died, I used to imagine I could see her face in the stars. This thought provoked a sudden question.

"Deon?" I asked.

"Yes Princess." Deon replied. He was kneeling by the fire, his horse legs bent under him.

"What was she like, my mother I mean, how was she to adults, and normal people?" I saw Deon's eyes glaze over, he was remembering.

"Just like you, so similar." Deon paused for a moment before continuing, he gazed at me longingly, like if he stared hard enough, I would become my mother. "I was maybe fourteen, fifteen, close to Hako's age. My parents were dead, my mother of a sickness, my father made one too many enemies. I was alone and ill, no money, no home, nothing. I came to the palace, I had nowhere to go. Then I saw her. I was begging in the gardens talking to some of the wood elves and I saw her on her walk. She was so beautiful, like my mother, but younger, so much like you. She came to me, I told her my story." Deon laughed slightly, his eyes watery. "Had the same soft spot for a youth with sad eyes and sob story as you, took me in, gave me a room in the palace, then when I was eighteen, I joined the army. I fought for years until she died. Then the king asked me to be your bodyguard. I said yes immediately. It was for her. I wanted to keep her daughter safe. I loved her so much, as a mother figure, as a benefactor." Deon sighed.

"I'm glad she did, otherwise I wouldn't have such a good bodyguard." I said warmly, seeing my mother's face in the stars and beginning to dream.

I dreamt I saw her in the stars. her face was smiling down at me talking,

"My darling, you've grown, you've become such a fine young lady."

I smiled, up at her, "Not as fine as you were."

The familiar disapproving look came across her face. "Don't say that." It was funny that her disapproving look was one of the clearest I could remember but her smile was sort of hazy. I pictured her face, skin darker than Hako's and long blonde hair, exactly my shade, I remembered when if we put then next to one another you couldn't tell where my hair began and Mother's ended It had been eight years, but I had not changed too much. I dreamt about her often and generally she sings, as she did almost immediately as I gazed at her face in the stars, the lullaby I loved so much. I blocked out everything else drawing in the words. It was an old elven tune and I loved it. I knew it all word for word.

*I wish I could have you forever my child,*
*I wish I could hold you and never let go,*

23

*But you must always sleep and for that night I am bereft.*
*That is why I kiss you goodnight, two kisses.*

*The first kiss goodnight is for you to keep*
*The last kiss goodnight is for me while you sleep.*

*So keep my kiss and I will keep yours,*
*Hold it forever in your mind,*
*As I hold mine,*
*A lover's kiss is a powerful thing*
*But a mother's kiss is ten times more so.*

*So treasure my kiss and hold it to you.*
*Then fall asleep with my kiss on your lips.*
*My child, sleep now, I shall leave you,*
*But with one last kiss for your night.*

The next morning Deon woke me.

"Only a few hours to Griffin mountain, we should get moving, and when we get up there be careful. Those mountains are hard on a horse. I should know." Storm neighed in agreement. Centaurs and Horses understood each other. In fact, in some cases they could almost communicate with one another. I clicked Storm to his feet and saddled him gently.

"You doing okay boy?" I asked as I swung onto his back. Storm jerked his head up and let out a loud roaring neigh before galloping off leaving Deon still putting out the campfire.

Griffin mountain was a sacred place. It wasn't for humans, or elves or centaurs or anything other than Griffins. Steep and rough with terrain you shouldn't brave without wings. Griffins hunt and live alone but they are all part of the Senate. A Senate is the collective noun for a

24

group of Griffins. They met when necessary and had a leader. The lead Griffin would be at the very top of the mountain, so we had to climb high. After a while it was plain, I couldn't ride Storm anymore. I dismounted and pointed him down the mountain.

"Take it easy boy." I instructed. Deon was struggling. He was using his hands far more than Centaurs usually did, gripping tight to damp cliff faces. Griffin mountain was desolate. No life existed on it apart from Griffins. That is why we only saw them when they came hunting. They lived in caves hence why we always tried to go under or over any Griffin cave we came across, even hanging onto the ledge by our fingertips and pulling ourselves across. At one point we had to walk past a cave. Luckily, the Griffin was asleep, curled up in the huge nest of twigs and feathers, it's wing over its head. After that it wasn't long before we reached the sharp peak of the mountain and entered the cave of the Alpha Griffin.

The Alpha was midway through a meal by the looks of it. His beak was bloodied, and the crushed form of a deer was lying before it. The Griffin looked up at me, his beady eyes flicked to Deon for a moment then looked me up and down, noting my imperial armour and cloak.

"Hello." I said tentatively stepping in. Griffin's can understand elven tongue though they cannot speak it. "Call your brethren, we elves are here to beg for your help." The Alpha gave me a long cool look, then threw back his great feathered head and cried a screeching, bellowing, ear spitting call. I heard the wings begin to flap. I felt the talons clicking down on the rocks. I knew they were coming.

It didn't take long before the entire Senate was assembled. There are about fifty full grown Griffins on the Mountain, a hundred or so if you count the cubs and

25

juvenile ones. Griffin Mountain is not the only habitat for the Griffins, but it is the biggest. The others who live in the woods are outcasts, sinners who have been thrown out of the Mountain for something they did. The Griffins all looked at me waiting for my piece, silent and deadly they stood cramped on the top of the mountain; mothers trying to keep their cubs in check, fathers chiding their sulky looking adolescents. Griffins are just like humans really, just like them. I cleared my throat and told them of Casseil and his army. I waxed lyrical on the chained and bound Griffin Casseil had rode in on. At this the Griffins' feathers bristled, their beaks snapped, and claws tensed.

"Please join us, ally with us and fight this brutal army, if not for the Elves and the other Creatures of Charyass then for your liberty."

The bird in a Griffin makes them ruthless, eager and self-serving, yet the lion makes them loyal, brave and courageous. The Alpha didn't need to talk to his brethren, he took one look at their ruffled feathers and beady black eyes hardened with a steely resolve, and he leapt to his feet letting out a battle cry louder than anything I'd ever heard before. He ruled the other Griffins calling for their allegiance and the reply was wholehearted and positive. Right before our eyes the Griffins took off streaming forward to the Palace, a sight so magnificent.

The Alpha was about to follow, taking off last to make sure everyone was alright.

A sudden thought sprung to mind. "Could you reach out to the Hippogriffs?" I asked. They bore a distant relation to the Griffins and the two could communicate quite well." The Alpha bowed his great head and nodded, then cried again, this time the pitch was lower, and the sound carried much, much further. then he was off. With one powerful flap of his wings he was gliding down towards the valley below.

26

The journey back wasn't too bad. Storm was quiet as was Deon. The night we camped we barely talked but when we passed the seafront Deon said.

"I'd hate to be a merman." I understood his meaning. The seas are plagued with Krakens, huge octopus, and squid creatures that could crush a ship in seconds. Luckily Krakens are rare and sleep out the majority of their lives, and when not, they are peaceful creatures with a playful side. But anger a Kraken and you're a dead man. On a brighter note there are the Hippocampi. They are beautiful half horse half fish beings, far friendlier than most land monsters. They will on occasion permit a merperson to hold their neck whilst they are dragged along. There were huge sea horses big enough to ride and serpents longer than a ship. It was said a species of Hydra was down there too; great three headed beasts. We know little of their bodies for in a passing encounter they never break the water and if they do, you won't live to tell the tale. Merpeople however have conflicting stories of catching a glimpse of the bodies, some tell that they are huge and muscular with legs. Others say it is just a serpent's body and yet more claim either tentacles or fins. I could go on forever. There is an exceedingly long list down there and the line between reality and myth with the merpeople is incredibly fine. To be fair we have truly deadly creatures on land too, like the Chimerae, a huge part lion part goat, part snake, creature. They are rare and live alone, generally in caves and if not in a cave, you're in trouble because they're probably guarding their babies. And then there are Manticores. not rare at all and desperately vicious, they don't care a bit what they eat and are happy to kill whatever comes in their way. There are also Minotaurs though they like to lurk in underground cave networks and aren't easy to find. Minotaurs are somewhat lacking in the brain and sight departments but when it comes to the smell of brutish strength and anger they are dominant. And who could forget dragons. Old wise and powerful, they look down at us as if we are their playthings and I suppose we are. Dragons can live hundreds of years; the really ancient species can make it to the thousands. Our lifetime to them is like the blink of an eye.

When we arrived back at the palace it had transformed. The valley was filled with the army, all training, preparing. Beasts were all around. Manticores hissed and snarled at passing soldiers. A Phoenix soared overhead; it's red and orange plumage rippled as if it were alight, breathing a swirl of fire out of its sharp beak. Hippogriffs and Griffins paced restlessly looking at the horizon where I could see a black line approaching. Merpeople were standing in the shallows on their fins, armed with tridents and nets. Wood elves were all armed and ready, with bows and daggers. Centaurs wore armour emblazoned with the sign of a bow, their weapon of choice, and two crossed swords, another weapon of choice. Satyrs trotted around on their shaggy goat legs wielding sling shots and clubs. Little Chamroshs scampered about, their dog's legs and hawks' wings and face making them below my waist in height, and in a way slightly cute. Somehow someone had found a Minotaur and it thudded around, it's heavy muscular bull's haunches shifted under the fur, the meaty slabs of muscle flexing and relaxing as it moved. The human or elven torso was covered with a thick pelt of black fur and the bull's head was huge, the nose sniffing constantly and the sharp horns swinging from side to side. And there were far more magical creatures around, but no Dragons. I hurried up to the palace with Deon behind me and jumped off Storm. A wood elf boy was on hand and grabbed hold of the Storm's reins. I ran through the gates and towards my father's chambers.

28

In Father's private meeting room, he was talking to Hako, when I burst in. They both greeted me with hugs and smiles.

"You did so well to bring us the Hippogriffs and the Griffins at the same time. I was very worried for you." Hako said,

"He's been scared stiff," Father jibed.

Hako protested. "I was not." I laughed and ruffled my brother's hair.

"So, what's the army like?" I asked.

"Which one?" asked Hako.

"Both."

Father sighed.

"Ours is strong; we have the willingness of all who serve in it and the power of freedom. We're organized and quite big." I predicted a however, I wasn't disappointed. "However, their army is brutal and huge, thousands of men, hundreds of captured elven archers; Dragons chained to ground made to breath fire; Centaurs branded and bridled; merpeople kept in tanks. It's monstrous. They're the real monsters not us." I sighed.

"How long till war starts?"

Father gestured to a letter lying on the table.

"A day. Just received this from Casseil."

I frowned,

"Casseil is the head of the army then?"

Father shook his head, his brow creased with thought and confusion.

"He seems high up in it but… read the letter, it should only take a few moments." I dutifully picked up the letter. The tone made me hate Casseil even more to start with, then it changed. The letter read.

*Dear Kallias, king of Elves,*

29

*We shall attack in a day. You have that long to join us and harness the power in your animals. That long, but if not, we will attack, and we will win. You will die. your kingdom will fall and your children will be left with nothing, and then after they've lost all they could think they had to lose, we will take what is the most important thing in our lives, more important than life itself I'd say because this is the essence of life; we will take their freedom. And mark my words Kallias, there is nothing that can prepare someone for slavery. Nothing on the planet. You have not felt true pain or loneliness or hardship until you are owned by somebody else and you are shackled and chained up to live out the rest of your miserable days.*

"I'd say Casseil is a slave." was my verdict after reading the letter. Father nodded in agreement as did Hako.

"The man sounds miserable." Hako said. "Who can channel that much spite without someone to be spiteful against?" I nodded in agreement.

"A day to prepare, are we going to be ready?" I asked. Father nodded.

"I guess so, we don't fight with the format we fight with heart."

I snorted.

"Heart might not be enough in the end, Dad."

As I walked through the palace grounds, I caught sight of Asir, dressed in battle armour with his hair swept back from his face, tucked behind his ears. Asir hooked up to me, he was holding his bow in one hand and one of his daggers in the other.

"You're back, I was…"

30

"If you dare say worried, I will make you eat that dagger." I snapped. Asir hurriedly tightened his grip on the dagger and stepped away.

"Then I was not worried. I knew you would get them there. I was missing you."

I laughed and nudged him playfully.

"You don't happen to know where I can find a telescope, to see the army better." I asked. Casseil's army had ground to halt about half a mile off. Asir nodded and beckoned for me to follow him. Soon we came to a white tent in which were tables full of maps and measurements, old weapons and bits of parchment. A she-elf stood in the center of it all her eyes bright and her long thick red hair a mess around her face.

"Thalia, this is Athena, the princess. She would like to borrow a telescope." Asir said with a bow. Then to me. "This is Thalia, one of our best scouts, and artists, she can draw anything she sees." Thalia looked at me. She was in her late thirties or so and her mouth curved into a smile when she saw me.

"Do you want me to talk you through the army, my tent has a great vantage point we can see them in detail, come." I followed, noting Thalia snatched up a telescope, a map and a piece of parchment with a drawing of something on it.

I sat on the hill watching the army through the telescope. Thalia's words began to explain it all to me.

"Right, now you are looking at the cavalry." I stared at men sitting astride centaurs. The Centaur's hands were bound with rope and their hair was being used to turn them in different directions. As no fighting was going on many men had dismounted. Leaving their mounts in a wooden pen with a trough of water in it. I saw an ugly black brand on the rump of one. I'd seen this custom with horses, but

31

never with such wise and sentient beings as Centaurs. The men riding them kicked at them like you would a stubborn donkey, yanking on their hair and slapping their sides. "Now the infantry is on the other side there." Thalia was saying. The infantry was even worse; Satyrs with their hands cuffed. Their slingshots were on the ground a while away from their pen which was blocked by cattle guards. They didn't have sufficient armour, just a breast plate and a feeble excuse for a helmet, to the men they were worth nothing. Some Minotaurs were in separate pens, sitting or lying on the floor moaning. A ring had been stuck through each of their noses, and they were also hemmed in by cattle guards, and heavy metal rails. Two Chimera were locked in separate pens, snarling to each other from the lion head, braying from the goat head, and hissing from the tail that was a snake's head. I kept the telescope moving and came across a burning forge.

"Are they?" I asked, looking closer.

"Yes, they are." Thalia confirmed, I stared at them moving around the furnaces banging metal with their powerful arms, their small bodies stripped to merely a loincloth. They were Dwarves.

Dwarves aren't native to Charyass. the climate isn't right for them. they thrive in two different areas depending on the species. This type of Dwarf from what I saw was the southern kind, their dark skin and shaved heads giving it away. They lived in the hot sweltering, rocky terrain of Swanyal far south of Charyass. It suddenly struck me how many kingdoms this army must have passed to have this array of creatures; many were not native to Charyass. The Dwarves shuffled along on their chains weighing them down. "They're being worked relentlessly, making hundreds of weapons a day." Thalia said, her tone steely. "Those humans are patrolling them like crazy. it's horrible.

Look at the Arial corps though." I dutifully turned and saw them. They were huge, a mess and tangle of flapping wings; screeching and roaring. I saw a Cockatrice, a huge, winged mix of a gargantuan rooster and a dragon. With two scaled clawed legs of a dragon and the same scaled and powerful tail and bat like leathery wings. But the head and neck were all rooster, a huge hanging wattle, crimson red and a high arching comb to match. The feathers were orange and yellow and blended almost seamlessly into the scales. The animal was bucking and squawking as the rider (whom I presumed to be a novice) struggled to keep it in check with its hard reins. I saw what looked like an officer riding a Manticore. I noted that the Manticore's tail had been encased in steel so it couldn't poison its tormentor. Griffins were curled up in pens, their saddles still on them. Hippogriffs trotted around their own pen, their muscular horse's hindquarters flexing and tensing whilst their eagles front pecked and tore at the metal netting that encased their pen to prevent them from flying away. But there were far more cages, and chains, far more pens and reins, the army was huge and desolate, and terribly intimidating.

# The Ancient Ones

I watched for a while longer, with Thalia answering a lot of my questions.

"So, do you know who their commander is yet?" I asked. Thalia nodded.

"I found out not two hours ago. Sent a messenger to your father. He calls himself Phaeton." I nodded slowly.

"Have you seen Phaeton?" Thalia shook her head.

"It wasn't safe. He had guards; so many guards." I understood. I was about to turn back to the army when I heard a polite cough behind me. I turned to see my old tutor Leas. Leas is a Satyr. His legs are white as is his hair and beard, crusted with age. His beard reached down to his belly and his face was wrinkled with laughter lines, and his small hazel eyes were kind. I leapt up and threw my arms around him.

"Oh Leas, you're back." When I was fifteen and Leas had taught me and Hako all he knew. He left, went into the woods to study and learn. Father built him a special house for his work and an observatory up in the mountains. Leas smiled.

"Yes Athena, your father sent word to me about this threat. He requested my advice, and if not advice, the honor to give me sanctuary, so here I am."

We left Thalia, and Leas and I began to walk through the gardens as we had so often done in my youth.

"You've grown so much in three years, my child." He said. His eyes were bright. I smiled. Leas winked at me. "And your father brought me up to speed on your long list of suitors." I laughed, then glanced around to make sure Asir wasn't nearby. Leas smiled and then sat down on a stone bench. It was the same bench we used to sit at together whilst he told me stories. "Your Father asked me to tell you about the old days." Leas said with a sigh. I nodded. These were some of my favorite stories. one of the things that I loved about them was that everything seemed so wild and dangerous. Even though Leas had lived over one hundred and fifty years, making him near eighty in human or elven years even his grandparents would not have been alive during the old days. Leas smiled and began. "It started with the sea. a raging torrent of black water, empty of any life, then slowly it began to fill, creatures of all kinds began to fill it and then they began to battle. During these battles, the sand from the sea was clawed up and land was created. Creatures came to the land. Soon it thrived itself, then humanoid creatures were created." The Creation myth is a short and garbled one. Nobody really tells it properly but it's something along those lines. Leas smiled and continued. "They were days of intense danger and savageness. The creatures were far worse than they are today. The sea was far more dangerous. You've heard of the serpents they have down there?" I nodded eagerly. I was suddenly a little girl again, enraptured by Leas's words.

"Yes, longer than a ship." I remembered. Leas laughed mockingly.

"Those serpents are nothing compared to the majesty and immensity of a Leviathan." My ears pricked up higher. I could feel the fine and delicate muscles in them do so. Elven ears are rather like dogs, they can twitch and turn to convey emotion for us. Right now, my ears were excited. Leas saw them and his face creased into a wide smile, then he continued. "A Leviathan is longer than an entire fleet of ships, and fast too. they can move through the water faster than any mermaid. Unlike Krakens, Leviathans go looking for trouble; highly territorial you will only find one every hundred miles of ocean. they like to have their distance.

35

When they were mating you could not go out to sea. Merpeople couldn't leave their sea caves, it was so dangerous. They mate violently. the sea wouldn't rest. it would churn like the wildest and most savage of storms with their tails thwacking and their bodies writhing and twining together. They weren't like the serpents of today. for one thing they had legs, powerful strong legs that they could walk on land with, that had claws that could grip a cliff face as it climbed out of the water. When a Leviathan was injured it would either climb onto land and seek out a mountain or a valley to rest, or it could swim into the largest cave it could find. A Leviathan would take up an entire valley just to lie full stretch. They'd have to wind their bodies around an entire mountain. they weren't built for land, nothing that big is built for land." I nodded. I was almost sad that the Leviathan had died out. Leas wasn't finished. "The sea also had Hydras." I frowned at him.

"Leas they still have those now." Leas shook his head,

"No now we have their relatives, three heads, three measly heads. in the olden days a Hydra would have seven heads, each independent each having their own personality. they all fought hard and would ambush victims by pretending to just be one serpent making the unfortunate animal run the other way to be met by another serpent then another then another, it was a little game to them."

"How did the number of heads go down?" I asked. Leas shrugged.

"I expect seven head attached to one body was a massive argument all the time, all wanting to do different things. they might quite literally tear themselves apart." The image was a little too literal for my liking and I grimaced.

"Were Kraken bigger in those days?" Leas nodded.

"A whole lot bigger, nowadays they're not too much bigger than two colossal squid. Capricorns and Hippocampus the same." Capricorns are rather like hippocampi except they are half goat instead of horse, "In fact in those days Capricorn were pretty lethal, Hippocampi have always been herbivores, non-aggressive, quite sweet really, but Capricorns were omnivores, vicious and stubborn, partial to some meat if they could get their hands on it."

Leas switched to the land animals after that.

"On the land things were just as rough, we were terrorized by all kinds of things. Behemoths, huge elephantine creatures with shaggy fur and tusks longer than trees. They towered higher than this hill, traveling in herds of about ten, peaceful usually. Herbivores eating trees, all the tree not just the leaves, the wood and the bark too. But if you annoyed one you would be stamped out of existence in minutes. We had pegasi all over in little herds. There were giants who were to a Behemoth like an elf would be to an elephant. And to a behemoth and elephant was the size of a mouse. Giants were so big and wise, but they existed in their own world up there. they lived in huge underground cave systems, that could accommodate their height. a lot like us, every family had their own cave and they were all connected and together a real community, what did they call it..." Leas searched his mind for a second. "A percussion. that is it a Percussion of giants. I'm barely scratching the surface of the ancient creatures Athena, there are far more." I smiled and nodded,

"How did they all go extinct?" I asked. Leas's face hardened and he took my hand.

"Now what I'm about to tell you I expect you to take seriously and not to laugh," I nodded earnestly. Leas took a deep breath and said,

"I believe they aren't all extinct."

I leapt up, my eyes popping, my ears probably twitching like crazy in a seriously embarrassing way. Leas laughed and patted the bench again.

"Athena hear me out. their numbers decreased. I can tell you that a Leviathan lives indefinitely until someone or something kills it. They have no predators and when they mate, they have at least two babies. The sea is vast but even it did not have room for the increasingly growing population of Leviathans. they began to have wars over territory, the sea began to grow barren of sea life. they had to prey on other monsters, juvenile Leviathan even, merpeople, anything. Soon they began to be seen less. Merpeople would find their corpses in trenches, slowly decomposing, the skeletons becoming their own little ecosystems you know, some mer villages are even built around them. Anyway, the numbers decreased. they became injured, but only a few hundred corpses were found, and Leviathans are survivors. even a Hydra probably couldn't kill one. I think they just migrated, further apart, some with bad injuries near fatal ones crawled onto land or into coastal sea caves to sleep for a few decades or centuries until the wound healed up." I realized that a Leviathan population completely dying out was seriously unusual and odd. How on earth would they do such a thing, who would kill them properly. Leas saw the realization on my face.

"Not all Hydra would be at war with each head. Some would live in peace, away from mer gossips and other creatures, somewhere where it isn't too hard to find food when they venture out of their home. Humans pulled down some giants, and scared others off. The Behemoths and Griffins took care of some, but for all we know they just disappeared further underground and left their carefully dug cave systems to the minotaurs, who may just be guarding the entrance to their true homes. They say Dragons hunted Behemoths to extinction. one Behemoth meal would last a dragon two or three years at least, and we don't have too many Dragons in Charyass. Pegasi can't have died out due to the fact their usual food became sick and all dyed out, their intelligent and creative creatures. I think they found another supply somewhere we don't know about. But we can find it." I was excited and I was surprised. I leaned into Leas. he spoke to me in a lower voice. "My father was a scientist like me. He drew a map. a map of last sightings of the ancient creatures. one was from my Grandfather." My eyes widened. and my voice was hoarse.

"Your grandfather saw an Ancient creature." Leas nodded.

"Everyone wrote him off as delusional from the wounds and blood loss, couldn't believe anything he said. He was just out fishing in his favorite bay. It was obscure he was the only one who knew about it. He'd caught a fine catch and he wanted to stop in a cave to have lunch. He stopped at one…" Leas's eyes clouded over. "He thought it was just small. He didn't realize it was alive. He started the fire and began cooking the fish. Then… then he saw the tail twitch. the monster unfurled itself, turning, flowing, stirring and writhing in the tight cramped space. Its coils seemed endless as did the cave. He couldn't run. Consumed with terror. Stuck still with fear and wonder. Finally the creature's head was facing him, and it opened it's huge eyes. They were the eyes of wisdom of knowing. He investigated their immense greenness and witnessed a phenomenon only known to the ancients. My grandfather saw the past in those eyes. He saw the reflections of the images of what this creature had been through, saw the wounds and the pain. He saw her children be devoured. Saw her be slashed and torn at. He saw her memories, and he couldn't move. He told me, he told me the animal was gentle with it, almost like it cared for our pain. He barely even noticed the claw

39

until it had slashed all along his side. Then my grandfather ran, or more accurately he hobbled. He thought the creature wasn't hungry or healed enough to give chase. I suppose he wasn't the only cloven creature to walk past unsuspectingly."

Leas took a weathered scroll from the leather satchel he was holding. I pulled it out and let out a low whistle. Leas's family must have an artistic trait, as he had always drawn pictures with me when I was a toddler. In fact, he'd taught me how to draw. Now I was almost as good as him. These pictures here, they were at the same level of detail. The map had creatures all over it. there was a Leviathan curled at the coastline. A hydra's many heads surfacing from the ocean, a huge Giant sitting on a cliff edge.

"Wow, Leas this is amazing, but why are you telling me this?" Leas pursed his lips, his grip on my hand increased and his brow creased even deeper with worry.

"Athena, we don't know what's going to happen, but your father, he thinks, if he doesn't make it through, he might... you might have to find these ancient ones, because they might be the only things that could save us."

# And So It Begins

That night I had dream, a restless dream plagued with darkness, I saw a charred landscape, a shell of a valley and the elven palace abandoned, overgrown with weeds and smothered in moss. The valley was ghostly quiet and void of movements. Suddenly at the forest edge there paced a marvelous creature, radiant and wonderful, long nimble legs and huge feathery wings. Eyes glittered from the equine head and the creature was the deepest ebony in colors. The Pegasus trotted smartly from the forest, somehow oblivious to the carnage around, smartly stepping over strewn rubble from the town below. I stared down at the animal, I'd always liked the idea of pegasi, during my youth riding one had been a common girlish fantasy, but I'd always been more interested in just watching them. The majesty and power were enthralling, "Gorgeous," I murmured, the animal's head turned to me instantly. The ancient gaze in the hazel eyes was wise and captivating. "Princess," I remembered it was merely a dream, my mind playing tricks but the reverent tones in the Pegasus's voice seemed very real,

"Yes?" I replied querying.

"This does not have to be how it ends," I shivered a cool breeze chilling me and gazed at the decrepit land. "Charyass?" I croaked almost disbelieving, this was not my home, this could not be my home,

"Maybe," the cryptic response was not especially useful.

"What? Why?" I murmured incoherently, an amused whiny called from the coal beast,

"War," was the blunt answer, "War and lack of wisdom." I shivered again,

"Lack of my wisdom?" I thought I perceived an almost imperceptible nod,

"Maybe." The Pegasus sounded concerned as their gaze stared at me, "But it doesn't have to be this," the wings the Pegasus unfurled were huge and powerful as it flew to where I stood. I guessed I was in the air maybe, I was so disoriented that I couldn't quite work out where I was, I could see everything without turning much, maybe it was just an illusion, my strange dream not prophetic, not prophetic.

"Please don't let this be prophetic," I muttered, the Pegasus whinnied again,

"Perhaps it isn't, this is only a future, not the future." I was not in the mind to nitpick the indefinite and definite article right now.

"What can I do to stop this?" I asked watching the Pegasus turn away, desperation crept into my voice, "What can I do?" The Pegasus moved fast it was nearing the forest edge when it whirled in the air to look at me,

"Fight well princess, and wisely." Around me the world faded as the Pegasus disappeared into the forest, the advice ringing in my ears.

I woke that morning to horns sounding, and when I sat up, I saw the form of Deon by my bed. I jumped and yelped. Usually Deon does not bother me while I am sleeping. He stays outside my door and takes shifts with the other guards so he can get some sleep.

"Oh, sorry princess." Deon said bowing. "Your father requested I take extra vigilance of you tonight. We are going to war." I hurriedly pulled on my armour and let Deon clip on my weapons. Elves do not fight with helmets. We wear hoods attached to our armour. I do not know why. Possibly something to do with the anonymous killer. The elven crest of a huge oak tree spread across my chest in black. Melissa braided my hair swiftly and I marched to my father's hall. on the way I bumped into Asir. he was completely ready for battle, his hood up,

"Oh hey, are you going out there?" I asked pointing at the lined-up battalions. Asir nodded sucking in his teeth.

"Hopefully, I'll make it through the first day." I smiled.

"Hopefully I am a good enough boss for that, and I might just need a second in command. If you are a good soldier, a promotion might be coming your way." Asir smiled and saluted.

"Yes, my lady, I like the sound of that." I gripped his hand tight.

"Please Asir, be careful out there. I have extra protection, but you are just a foot soldier. you aren't going to get much attention." Asir smiled and leaned in closer, suddenly I was aware of the prying eyes of Hako and I cried.

"Yes! If I died, we'd have a problem because a moron would be the heir to the throne." Hako approached and I gently detached myself from Asir wishing him luck and followed Hako away.

"So, did you choose for him to be under your command or was it a coincidence?" Hako asked as we walked.

"I chose. I like him." I asserted. Hako nodded.

"Well that's plain," the comment was pointed, and I flashed back to Asir's face.

"What's the problem? You think it's all happening too fast?" I asked, rolling my eyes.

"No, we just have somewhere to be and too many eyes were watching." Hako replied "Anyway I was passing through and I thought we could walk together like we used to." I remembered walking to training with Hako, Deon and Tull, who was Hako's bodyguard, trotting behind us. I shrugged.

43

"Well that's sweet but we're about to go to war so having a good relationship with me is the least of your worries."

Father looked worried when we met him. He was dressed for battle and his eyes looked wild and scared.

"Are we ready?" The question was not addressed to us. General Vida was standing before our father. Vida was one of the highest and strongest generals in all Charyass and one of father's main advisors.

"Yes my king, as ready as we'll ever be." Vida curtseyed and swept out of the room upon our entry. Father turned to us.

"Battle starts soon, you two need to be on top form, we need to win this, and we need to win it with minimal cost to our army." I nodded.

"Yes father, we will try, are you fighting today?" I asked. Father shook his head.

"I shall observe, the least my people need is for their king to be wounded before the first day is over. Deon, Tull, I must request you ride into battle at my children's sides, I know this is above and beyond what you are hired for, but I need to keep my children safe." Deon nodded.

"Anything for Athena, my king. I swore to Hermia I would give my life for her child." Tull bowed, one of his legs bent his head inclined.

"Yes, I shall ride alongside Hako and fight for him and with him." Father smiled and stood.

"In that case, please escort my children to the battlefield, and carry my blessings with you."

I sat on a storm watching the line of humans and chained animals in front of me. Hako was nowhere to be seen. his regiment was a while away. I felt entirely alone, my foot soldiers were restless and eager. The few mounted officers were stern and grim, and I was scared. Storm snorted and jerked his head around. Deon gave him a calming look. The horns sounded once again. Suddenly Storm was moving, and around me soldiers were screaming war cries and I was scared. Creatures were cawing and roaring, screeching and bellowing, and I was scared. Our opposition was on the move too. Humans charged their centaurs forward, above beasts clashed together and I was scared. Men fell before my eyes, and I was horribly, nerve bendingly, heart stoppingly, blood freezingly, mind numbingly, scared.

# Stories, Changes, Losses

The fighting was brutal. I cut down endless fighters but was careful to try and spare the centaurs and creatures they rode. Unfortunately, a rider less centaur could not move due to their chained hands. It would be swept up by a foot soldier and mounted. Deon was beside me all the way, until I felt Storm groan. I saw a Satyr below me, their slingshot resting in its hands. Storm's leg was bleeding and he was stumbling. I drew my bow and pulled an arrow to the quiver in moments. the Satyr fell to the ground with an arrow through its eye. Storm groaned and buckled. Deon swiftly pulled me up onto his own back and grabbed hold of Storm's bridal. The centaur's superhuman strength lifted the entire horse to his feet and began to gently lead it back through our soldiers. We soon found a mare rider less, standing alone. I climbed onto her back and let Deon go with Storm,

"I'll be back soon princess." Deon said. I nodded and wheeled the new horse around, charging forward.

I fought without mercy, leading the charge. My new horses did not feel fear either. She just ran. She was a beautiful dappled grey mount with honest, intelligent eyes, just like Storm. I tried to put him out of my mind. Deon would take care of him. Deon would get him to a healer. And this horse would do for now. She neared Storm's intuitive recklessness and reliable determination. In short she was as like me as Storm was. I felt a hand at my leg and was about to strike with my dagger when I saw the elven hood. Asir peered out from underneath it. His arm was bleeding, though it seemed to just be a flesh wound and his face was bruised above his right eyebrow.

"What's up?" I said, kicking away a human and hauling Asir up behind me.

"You don't need to do this Athena, I'm fine down there." he protested.

"Yes, but if you want to chat this is the best way to do it. Just have your bow knocked all the time." Asir nodded, then looked down.

"What happened to Storm?" When I tensed he looked away,

"Oh sorry. This horse seems okay. What's her name?" I shrugged.

"Not a clue. I will see if anyone recognizes it after the battle. We're not doing too well are we?" I pointed to our retreating battalions, being easily pushed back by the onslaught of brutal fighters. Asir nodded.

"When will they stop?" I shrugged.

"I reckon pretty soon. We're almost into the village." As if I had commanded it, the army suddenly stopped and, apart from one long line, all went back to their camp. They seemed to be bringing it forward. We sulked back to our camp, passing dead bodies all around. Asir jumped off my horse, back to join the infantry and I climbed the hill to the palace. The palace was filled with soldiers and the wounded. I was heading to the animal healing sanctuary when my father saw me. Father ran forward smiling with relief, then he stopped.

"That horse!" his voice broke, and his eyes widened, "Where did you find it?" His tone was urgent, and I swung my legs over and off the mare's back.

"On the battlefield. Storm was wounded and Deon took him to the sanctuary, Father? What's the matter?" Father sighed and traced a hand down my mare's face.

"That horse belonged to general Vida." Understanding flooded through me and I hugged my father.

47

"It's okay, she might still be out there, Vida is a strong fighter and a survivor, she might just be hiding, or she might have been taken prisoner." Father nodded,

"It doesn't matter whether she's alive or not, my personal feelings don't matter, what matters is that she's not here to lead and we need her to do that." I nodded then smiled as the mare neighed.

"Did she give this mare a name?" I asked. Father nodded.

"She said it was the best of horses, Vida called her Luna." At hearing her name, Luna reared up showing a curve of black hair on her chest.

"I will ride her until we find Vida or until Storm gets better. She's a fine mount." I proclaimed. Father nodded as I waved over a stable boy.

"Put this horse in the empty box next to Storm. Brush her and wash her thoroughly. Take extra care as if this were Storm." Father said sternly. The young elf nodded and took the reins. He tossed a triumphant look over at another stable boy nearby who was empty handed. I smiled at the petty innocence of normal children, children who did not have to rule a kingdom or fight a war when they were older.

Storm was lying on a bed of straw, his body coated in a cold sheen of sweat, a she-elf was crouched at one of his forelegs, the weeping wound still gushing blood. Deon was there too. He greeted me with a relieved smile and then turned back to Storm.

"The wound was already infected when I brought him. Also, they think the stone might have broken a bone." I knew the weight of this. If his bone was broken, it meant that he would have to be put out of his misery. I threw open the stable door and ran to his head.

"Hey boy." I said softly holding him. "You're going to be okay. I'm going to do absolutely everything I can to keep

48

you alive and well, alright, you're the best horse I've ever had, and you charged the best today." Storm's eyes looked up at me with love and understanding. I noticed his mane was still braided and folded into those small knots all down his neck and I gently began to undo them one by one. Soon his mane fell in a long free curtain of black. I did the same to the long, deft tail braid and smiled. He looked better now, freer. Suddenly the healer gasped and looked at Deon knowingly. Deon trotted over and knelt, bending all four legs.

"Princess." The healer said, her voice grave. "There is a break."

I tied the blindfold loosely around Storm's eyes, then I hugged him, breathing in his scent, his feel, his sound, one last time.

"Goodbye boy." I whispered hanging onto the great neck like I was fifteen again, jumping up to see my new birthday present. It had only been three short years, three short years of our life together, and now it was over. I felt the briny taste of tears in my mouth and then I stepped away, looking one last time. Storm was fully brushed and washed; his coat gleamed like it always did. His hooves were oiled and washed. His leg had been strapped up so he could stand for his last few seconds, like the proud horse he was. Then after drinking him in that one last time I ran away. Like a little child I ran back to my chambers into the strong, protective embrace of Deon. After a moment I heard the twang of the arrows, five archers fired at once, for an instant death. There was not a single cry of pain from Storm and I was proud of him for that, proud of him for being the strong proud horse he always was and always will be.

The next morning, I was woken by Deon to the news I would not be required to fight today,

"What!" I yelled at Deon.

"The king says, he doesn't expect you to fight today, not with the loss of Storm still weighing on you." I hurriedly began dressing, putting on my armour.

"Well you can just tell the king that they need all the help they can get, or does he think we won the last battle, and where is my bow?" I turned to see Deon held my bow high above his head.

"The king expected this, and he now demands it." I glared at Deon.

"As Princess Athena of Charyass, heir to the throne of Charyass, and your charge I command you to give me that bow!" Deon smirked and chuckled.

"If you laugh at me again, I'll have you sentenced to death." I yelled rashly. Deon laughed heartily then and said:

"Take this up with your father Athena, it's not my job." I glared daggers at Deon then turned and said:

"Fine, can you send for Asir, then have him come to my chambers and where's Melissa?"

Melissa did my hair the way she usually does it when I must join my father in court, and I wore a black dress. Asir arrived in armour, his hood down.

"Hello, you pulled me out of the front line, what's so important?" He asked. His arm had been bandaged and he had washed and cleaned thoroughly. In his freshly shined and polished armour, he looked as if he had never been to war.

"Hey." I said with a sad smile, suddenly Asir noticed my black dress and bowed his head.

"Oh Athena, I'm sorry about Storm. This evening I would be honored to attend his burial." I nodded.

"Yes, he was the best horse I've ever had; a birthday present when I turned fifteen, he... he was related to the mare my mother died on." Asir's eyes widened.

50

"I don't know how your mother died. I was young when it happened, only about…"

"Ten," I supplied, Asir nodded,

"Yes ten. The queen's death meant little to me, and it isn't exactly talked about much here." I nodded and patted my bed.

"Sit, time for a story."

"My mother was a warrior, an adventurer, but she had to rule alongside my father, and she loved her children. One day a messenger came from Metalk, you know a trading town in the hills. He said they needed a favor. Turns out they had an injured Dragon laying waste to their lands. It was awful. They needed our help direly. They needed someone from the capital to send out troops. Mother said she would go with a small guard. She said it would be fine; they just needed to have the right medical equipment to heal the dragon. Dragons understand us and they know when we are trying to help. My father agreed, he always trusted my mother, even against his better judgement. The journey was easy, but when they arrived, they found the villagers trying to build walls to keep the dragon, which was pretty much land bound due to its torn wing. My mother approached it. It was working well until suddenly the Dragon reared up and blew a plume of fire right at her. A villager let fly a makeshift catapult. He was scared for her, but the missile hit my mother first. The Dragon was shot and killed with arrows by the small group of soldiers that had been brought along, but the villager who killed her ran off the mountain and jumped down towards the lake. He died. When they brought her home, she had an amazing funeral. All of the valley were silent the moment her ashes were scattered. The entire army shot flaming arrows into the air; imagine it, thousands of arrows all flying into the air. She wanted them scattered in her favorite glade and so we did. It is beautiful down there. Butterflies and deer, fish in the creek that look like living sunbeams. She used to take me there. Anyway, that's how she died." I finished my story with a sigh, trying to clear my eyes of the unshed tears that began to swim in them, then stood up. "Look I shouldn't have pulled you away from battle just to tell you about my mother and mope about Storm. If you want to you can go back." Asir nodded,

"Yeah, that might be better," He said smiling nervously as he hurried out of the room.

"How many deaths so far king?" Asked Macos. We were in the hidden glade. It was late at night and a war council had commenced. All the advisors and high officers were there. Captain Sophia stood. Sophia was tall and blonde with bright blue eyes.

"We can confirm at least a hundred, but around fifty others are missing or in a critical stage with their injuries. I must also ask if we are treating Vida's case as a death or that she is missing because we are shorthanded, and it may be time to replace her." A few lesser Officers sat up a little straighter and tried to look as worthy for the position as possible. Father nodded.

"I have considered that angle and as we are in a critical situation and she has also contributed so much to this effort I have made my decision as to who to replace Vida with." Everyone looked eager, especially Sophia. She was the obvious choice, only a few rungs down from Vida, she was a great officer and warrior. "I am naming you a general…" Father was stringing this out deliberately I could see how he loved the suspense. "Princess Athena."

The war council was silent. Enraged looks began to cloud every face. Sophia flushed bright red and by the looks of it almost said something she would regret before nodding and sitting back down. It was Macos who spoke. As usual he thought just because he and Father had been childhood friends, he could say whatever he wanted.

"My king, do you not see how your daughter lacks hugely in experience. In fact, she has not even been through the usual training. Do not put this kingdom in jeopardy just because you can't say no to your daughter's puppy eyes." The room was silent, the tension building. Father gave Macos a long cool look,

"General Macos," He said slowly. Macos saluted smartly, the colour beginning to drain from his olive skin, "Would you like to face my daughter in one on one combat?" Macos shook his head.

"No sir." Father nodded.

"Are you king?"

"No sir." Father nodded again.

"Then I'll give you a choice. Either you apologise to my daughter and sit back down, or I dismiss you." Macos nodded.

"I apologise Princess. I was merely surprised and tired, due to these uncertain and strange times. I'm sure you will make a great General like Vida before you. And sometimes we all need some changes in our lives."

# Papering Over Cracks

"Well congratulations, General," Hako grinned, throwing his arms around me.

"I still command my battalion, though. By the way, that Macos is a total piece of Manticore Venom." I said as I watched Macos pass with his little servant elf whispering into his ear about something. "He absolutely hates me." Hako shrugged.

"Yeah of course he does. He hates me too. He thinks Father is too distracted by us, in his mind our handmaids, bodyguards, tutors and trainers should take care of all the raising, he should just see us occasionally and get on with ruling." I nodded as Hako and I walked together. We did not say where and I do not think either of us really knew but we just kept walking through the little huts and houses of the palace and everything. "So how was Storm's burial? I'm sorry I missed it, but I needed to get a cut on my leg bandaged, if I'd got there a minute later it would have been infected." Hako looked worried as if I were going to berate him for missing it but I just shrugged.

"He's at peace. I miss him, but Luna is good, and she can carry me through the rest of this war." Hako nodded,

"Yes, I'm sure she can." Suddenly we both stopped. Our walking had brought up to the highest point on the hill, up high above the valley and we could look down. Gone was the object of peace and virtue I had seen just days earlier, and in its place was a terrified symbol of war. No merpeople frolicked, no Centaurs showed off and no she elves flirted. Hako pointed to a long line of troops marching towards the front line.

"Look there from Metalk, young men and women volunteering, and over there." His finger strayed to another line streaming down the opposite hill, "They come from Haynol. People are coming to help, but I don't think they'll be enough." I nodded knowingly. We were on very thin ice. One crack and we would fall through.

"The civilians are fragile and scared. We need a morale boost." I suggested. Hako nodded.

"But how exactly are we meant to pull that off?" I opened my mouth to tell him I did not know when an idea sprang swiftly and brilliantly to mind.

"I know exactly how. Where's father?" Hako shrugged.

"In his chambers I suspect, why?" I grinned and turned away.

"Come on then, I know how to get people's spirits up." Hako smiled, he trusted my ideas more than I did.

"A parade?" Echoed Father wearily rubbing his face,

"Yes, the cavalry, the infantry, all of them. We could even persuade the creatures to do it. It would show our strength and our freedom is still very much intact." Father nodded.

"I agree with Athena, I'll send the order now. Tomorrow we shall not battle, we shall parade." Hako stepped forward,

"But Father won't that give them an opening to attack?" Father shook his head.

"They think they're going to win in a matter of days. They have all the time in the world. Every time we fight, they push us back further, we're on our knees and they'll give us time to beg."

"This would do nothing permanent King, it would in effect be a bandage for an ever-bleeding wound, we'd just be papering over the cracks in their feelings." Father nodded to the advice of the Officer in the war council,

"Yes, but it is the best we can do for now, paper over a few more cracks. Now I have informed you of all the

55

proceedings tomorrow. I expect you and all your regiments to be looking up to the part, shining and smiling. You are all dismissed." The council left but Macos stayed, I stared at him slowly returning to my seat.

"Is there something you wish to say to us?" I asked. Macos gave me a steely look.

"Princess, I have a matter I would like to discuss with your father." He spoke in the way he used to when I was a child. I half expected him to say, "Now why don't you go and play while the adults have a little chat." Luckily Macos proved himself to be above that though the slight opening of his mouth before he bit it back showed it had crossed his mind. Father looked at me.

"Athena, go get started with organizing parts of the parade, you came up with it, I would like to have you in charge." I nodded and bowed.

"Yes, thank you father. General." I nodded to Macos. Making his title sound as much like an insult as possible. before gliding out of the glade.

I did not leave in the slightest, stealing round in the woods surrounding the glade I scaled a tree. As the bark and moss smeared against my dress, I thought of what Melissa would say then ignored it and looked down on my father and Macos.

"Your majesty, I am coming to you as a friend, you need to hear this, the council aren't happy, the Officers and generals are in a state of shock and distrust, this decision to put your daughter in such a position of power whilst she is still so young, they aren't pleased." Father shrugged.

"They should get on with their work, you know winning the war." Macos nodded.

"Yes, sir I understand but they cannot win the war if their king is not ruling right, and that's what they believe. Look I do not think it is really your daughter they have a problem

56

with. I think it's far more likely to be her personality and history." Father glared at Macos.

"What is wrong with my daughter's personality?" Macos stepped back.

"Kallias," Macos looked like it wasn't even a question, "Her past string of lovers, her newfound relationship with this soldier. They aren't happy with a teenage girl, clearly prone to mood swings and letting her feelings cloud her judgement to be in this position." Father shrugged.

"Well Macos they'll just have to deal with it because right now I have a very small circle of who I can trust, and my daughter qualifies. On another note have you sent the search parties yet?" Macos nodded.

"Yes, after it was confirmed her body had not been found on the battlefield. I sent a small team of ten men to search for Vida. hopefully, they'll find her and bring her in fast." Father nodded and smiled.

"Yes, thank you Macos, now please leave me. I have a lot to think about." As Macos left I slowly climbed down the tree and lightly ran back to the chambers.

"Quite the turn out isn't it." Deon commented as I jumped up onto Luna's back and accepted the banner from him.

"Yes, it is. I still think Father should be leading the parade though. He is king." Deon shrugged.

"Well he's not, so just be happy he let you." I grinned.

"Believe me I am."

Luna trotted beautifully. she really cleaned up quite well. She had been in a sorry state when I had rescued her from the battlefield but now freshly scrubbed and with her mane braided and tied up, she really looked the part. The wind fluttered the banner well as it streamed out behind me, and the following troops all marched smartly along. The

57

Griffins were stalking proudly, and other animals marched as well. The people who were not fighting cheered and watched. We never force anybody. They can join if they want to and if they pass the physical and medical tests. And you must be over sixteen. As we marched and the band played, I felt like we could win the war, like we had a fighting chance. That's when the arrow came.

I saw it whizzing through the air. in seconds I had its target and in seconds I knew what to do. I threw my body forward, low, Luna began to gallop, and I felt the arrow pass over my neck. The fine hairs stood up on end and a chill shivered down my spine. There was uproar behind me. I heard the hooves of Deon, galloping to my aid. the entire army suddenly mobilized. There was shouting and screaming. somebody pointed to the woods and I saw a flash of a deep crimson cloak. I turned Luna and urged her towards the sniper. I heard Deon's voice.

"Princess, I must insist you wait... Princess, please. Your majesty. Athena, stop!" I did not listen, and I heard him galloping towards me.

"Come on Luna." I whispered.

"Let's see if you can outrun a Centaur, shall we?" The wood was dark and cold. I saw the running figure quite far away, weaving between trees. Luckily, Luna was agile. she slipped and bent round and over, ducking and jumping through the forest. I felt somehow that Vida had taken her through many times. I heard Deon was still hot behind me. He was coming closer, with his transport actually part of him he could make a better headway, due to the fact he could treat this wood like a normal run whereas to me it was a ride, and I had to trust Luna. As soon as I was close enough, I grabbed my bow and reached for an arrow. Soon it was leveled and ready. then the figure stopped turning to me. The face was obscured by a heavy hood but the eyes

58

gleamed, staring straight at me a bright solid blue that seemed to almost glow.

"Listen to this Athena. Your kingdom will fall, and your people will turn against you. So, prepare, for today is the beginning of the end." An elven arrow shot passed me and the man turned away flicking his cloak up to block the missile. Then he ran away.

Deon grabbed me and lifted me right off Luna and into his muscular arms, clicking his tongue at Luna to go back to the camp and glared down at me.

"That could have been so dangerous Athena. He just tried to kill you. What do you think would have happened if he tried to do it again? You aren't wearing battle armour, just this ceremonial stuff. He could have killed you." Deon's eyes were glazed with angry tears. "Do you know what that would have done to the kingdom? Do you know what that would have done to me?" I bowed my head. Deon had not scolded me like this since I was a child and it was frightening. Suddenly Deon stopped and just galloped back to the valley gripping my body tightly holding me close to him as if I was a newborn baby.

Father greeted me and Deon his eyes wild with fear and anguish his mouth set hard. Hako shadowed him and as Deon set me down, I was swept up again by my father and examined all over for wounds.

"You're alive." Hako stated. I smiled.

"It would appear so wouldn't it," I joked, Hako grinned slightly then Father smiled at Deon.

"Thank you for bringing her back Deon. please escort her back to her chambers and get another guard to help you keep watch over her. Don't let her out."

I sat in my room writing. I like to write when I can't leave. It is calming and transporting, a bit like reading. I was writing a short poem about a Leviathan curled up in its cave, brooding and trying to heal itself, trying to forget the pain. I was only halfway through when there was a sharp wrap on my door.

"Come in." I sighed, and Deon trotted in. He was still obviously angry with me as he did not say anything more than.

"Princess there is a war council." he left, leaving Melissa in his wake. Melissa smiled at me shyly, this caused me to look at her more. Melissa had been my handmaid since I was about fifteen, before her my handmaids had been required to take more of a nurturing role, more of a motherly figure instead of just a servant. We talked often yet I knew extraordinarily little of her, our discussions were usually about current events or just small talk, she had never volunteered any of her personal information.

"Melissa?" I began thoughtfully my brow creasing, "Where do you hail from?" Melissa looked away shyly, her hair fell over her eyes, it was ebony black, elegant and extraordinarily long as if it had not been cut in a long while, stretching to the small of her back. Though pulled out of her face by a portion of it being held up and tied back the rest hung loose. Her eyes were a stormy grey and oval. Her mouth was set firm and hard. Her cheekbones were high, and her face was thin, almost malnourished. She was dressed as usual in white, the respective dress of a handmaid, sometimes she had come with a headscarf on though some days not. Melissa appeared to have no intention of answering my query instead busying herself with my wardrobe, sifting through the trousers, dresses, tunics, shirts and jackets it held. "Melissa, I asked you a question." I repeated more firmly, Melissa nodded picking an emerald dress and laying it out.

60

"It's not important Princess really, you should be dressing for the council." I glared at her.

"We have over an hour, and if you don't tell me I'll make it an order." Melissa nodded then took a tentative seat on a chair.

"I was born in a small elven fishing town on the coast," I nodded with a smile.

"And how did you come to be here, surely you would have had a future there, a steady straightforward life." Melissa smiled fondly as if imagining what could have been.

"Yes princess, I could have had a very straightforward life but since I was born fate was set for me to have anything but that. I sense you wish to hear the story?" I nodded eagerly.

"Yes, I do."

Melissa insisted I put on the dress before she began. Once that was done, she made me lie flat on my bed. Making sure I wouldn't crease my dress too much.

"Fishing villages inhabited by elves are never rich. The merpeople fish far better and in far greater numbers so they provide most of the fishing produce for the inland cities, so we were poor. I had four sisters. We all looked terribly similar and I think my father was thankful we were so mentally different because after he came home from a day's work, tired and worried he wouldn't have been able to tell us apart. I was the youngest but one. I was labelled by my sisters as the obedient easy going one. I always obeyed my parents if they directed an explicit demand to me, but I was also happy to run along with my sisters and play or dare together. I was always truthful too. Then there was the eldest, Dahlia. Dahlia was envied by us all, as she was the smartest and most desired by all the other men in the village, and so well-mannered and graceful that if guests ever came my mother always had them meet Dahlia first. After Dahlia came Helena. Helena was levelheaded and practical, boringly so, we would say if she was being annoying. She was the goody two shoes or at least that's how Sara would scorn her. Sara was a year older than me, the middle child exactly and was often ignored by our parents. Sara took advantage of this, soon blossoming into a boisterous, daring, rebellious child, always getting into trouble and dragging us in after her. Then there was me and after that Nooria, she was the baby, meek and soft hearted, gentle and easily frightened." Melissa broke off her eyes clouding slightly, and her face seemed startled as if she had not thought about it in years. But she bravely continued. "Our father didn't have much to do with raising us, he'd fish from before dawn till after sunset, but our mother did help raise us though after each of our tenth birthdays more freedom was given and we could run about the village, doing as we pleased. Once Nooria was ten we could all run together, life was good we had all we wanted and it was all straightforward and easy just as you said." Once again Melissa broke off pushing her hair behind her delicate ears which flicked as the hair brushed them. "When Dahlia was twenty-one a man asked for her hand in marriage. Well, a man she liked asked her for her hand in marriage, others had done so before. There were few women in the community, far more men and Dahlia was the most loved, not only beautiful but intelligent and vocal, she also possessed an alluring wit and charm that people could not resist. Anyway, after Dahlia was married, we were a sister down, it felt like we were missing something. Then the sudden death of our mother did not help. But more tragedy soon came upon us for the fish in our area became scarce one fateful year. We had barely enough to feed ourselves now. Then the reason for our famine became clear. A woken Kraken descended upon the village. Kraken attacks

62

are rare. They are usually placid but someone had angered this one and it tore the village up, ripped the houses out of the ground and throwing them to the sea. My sisters and I escaped. We took Dahlia with us, though her husband and our father stayed with the other stupid villagers, trying to show their bravery and boldness by attempting to fight the beast and rescue the other villagers. I'm sure you don't need me to spell out for you what became of them." Melissa's face was now angry, and tears dripped slowly from her burning eyes. "Stupid so stupid." She muttered under her breath. "The journey here was long and with many bends and turning points, we had to leave Nooria and Helena in a highland city a while away called Yarren. Then Dahlia found a centaur and fell hugely in love with him. She told me she knew now that she hadn't loved her first husband but she did love the Centaur and as Dahlia was perfectly happy to have no children she left us until it was just Sara and me. We were together until we got here. We started together as servants when you were about ten. By the time you were fifteen, I'd worked my way up quite high and got the position as handmaid to the princess. Shortly after that Sara was fired and ran off. I don't know where to but I suspect back to one of our other sisters. Sara is a survivor. I can guarantee she's fine." I sighed at the end of the sad and yet somehow uplifting tale of love, tragedy and recovery.

"Are you never sad, do you never miss them?" I asked, Melissa laughed.

"Every day of my life I miss them Athena. I miss my home I miss my friends and my family. I grieve for them every moment. My hair is a sign of grieving. In the fishing villages you never cut your hair after a tragedy. If you're truly hurt by an event, you pay an homage to it by never cutting your hair. It was already long and now it's even longer. I so miss them but I hold it together. I have little moments of joy, temporary glue for my life, a few happy thoughts binding the grief and the pain."

# Desperate Measures

Suddenly Deon tapped on the door and as I sat up. Melissa caught sight of my hair still loose and free over my shoulders.

"Oh my, Athena come here I must try and do something with your hair!" I shook my head bouncing up.

"I'll be fine Melissa don't worry; I can look however I want; I am the Princess." Melissa looked at Deon helplessly and he nodded sternly.

"Yes, she is the Princess, and she seems to pick and choose when she wants to be the Princess and when she wants to be a regular, irresponsible, impulsive, adolescent."

I galloped Luna down the hill and practically sprinted to the glade where I grabbed my crown and hurried into the glade. Eyes followed me disbelieving as I marched through to my seat. I must have looked quite a sight, my hair flying loose and wild, my eyes bright, my cheeks flushed and my crown slightly askew. Father gave me a stern angered look that read. "We'll talk after." Then turned to the rest of the council.

"Now we're all here I think I should make you all abreast of the true happenings of today's parade. My daughter leading the parade was almost killed. Her quick reactions saved her from the arrow and she then tore off after the shooter. Her bodyguard went with her but they were unable to capture the assailant, the description of the man from what we could tell from under his hood fits with the main trait of Phaeton the leader of the human army, mainly burning blue eyes that are eerily lit, as if by magic. This Phaeton is highly mysterious and dangerous it would seem, and does not shy away from the action himself. Now we aren't doing well. I know the war is in its early stages but we are losing soldiers, a lot of soldiers, too many a day. Our troops have been diminished as if we'd been fighting for a year. We need ideas and I am open to any." The Council was silent for a moment then an Officer stood up.

"I propose a scouting mission sir, not just from far away, right into their camp see how they work, see if we can get a proper visual of Phaeton." Father snapped his fingers,

"Yes, you are a genius, now any volunteers?" Nobody volunteered except me. I shot my hand up and Father smiled. "It seems my daughter actually possesses bravery, and you ask why I made her general. Athena I will not let you go alone. Do you have a companion you'd like to choose?" I smiled.

"Yes, father I'm sure Asir will be more than happy to join me. I must emphasize that Deon would be far too noticeable so cannot come." Some of the Officers snickered but immediately ceased after a glare from both me and Father. I was surprised Macos wasn't making a fuss then I saw the malice glittering in his eyes and understood. He thought I'd be killed and then the outspoken and problematic princess would be no more, he thought Hako would be more flimsy or at least more traditional even if he wasn't manipulatable. Father smiled.

"Wonderful, does anybody oppose this move?" Nobody spoke. Macos positively beamed.

"No sir." He grinned. Father did not notice and turned to me.

"You leave tomorrow night. Tell Asir to be ready, and be very careful Athena, do not make noise, do not confront. Just listen and look, okay, listen and look." I nodded,

"Got it father. Listen and look."

The rest of the meeting was usual, discussions on losses and tactics placement and reinforcements. Once everybody

66

departed, I was left with my father and his eyes were daggers.

"Do you know why I made you a general Athena?" he asked coldly.

"Umm… because you think I have leadership skills and that I'm responsible." Father nodded.

"Exactly, because you are responsible, and you didn't seem that today, firstly hightailing after Phaeton then showing up both late and unkempt, you are meant to be a symbol of the grace, careful strength and wisdom of the royal family and you don't show that." I was suddenly angry. I didn't want to be a symbol I wanted to be a person and a princess who would one day rule.

"I am not a showpiece, you can't just give me some fake power and make me a symbol of how great you are, what's next is Hako going to become a Lieutenant, in case you didn't notice he's trying to have a childhood and I'm trying to have a life. And don't you start up about Asir again because I can love whoever I like!" Father glared at me.

"Don't ever dare to speak to your king and your father with such impertinence again. You are allowed to love whoever you want, and I wasn't going to touch on Asir I am however going to touch on the fact that you seem to not possess a verbal filter and the way you treat some of the other officers, they are good and respectable so what if they show disrespect you shouldn't. You may not like it, but you are still a child in many eyes, and you are going to need to prove yourself not to be. I would not have made you a general if the times weren't so dire, neither would I be allowing your little excursion, but desperate times call for ever more desperate measures and this is one of those." The words pulled me out of my strop.

"We're really losing, aren't we?" Father nodded.

"Yes, I'm afraid we are, we may need to try and find the dragons." I frowned at him thoughtfully.

"What is it with you and Dragons? You seem frightened of them, they're intelligent and peaceful, they will help if they understand the cause." Father nodded and he suddenly looked regretful, incredibly regretful and sad like he was eating himself up inside.

"Athena," he said quietly. "Have I ever told you about Tike."

Of course, I had never heard of this Tike and I was eager and ready to hear more, very eager and very ready. I leaned forward. Two mysterious stories in one day. That was interesting. Father smiled fondly at my eagerness and twitching ears just as Leas had done, that seemed like so long ago. Father looked so sad and so angry with himself as he told the story.

"I was young, younger than Hako I think, though not by much, I befriended a Dragon, same stage of his life as me, in his sixties or so." Dragons can live thousands of years and become full grown at age one hundred so this Dragon would have been in their teens. "We'd play together on a cliff edge; young dragons can be great playmates. I called him Tike, as in little Tike, ironically, I thought it was funny. One day I was boasting to my friends, Macos included, and someone asked if I could ride him, I told them no, said it was not right for an elf to ride a dragon unless specifically invited. They mocked me that day and told me I was a weakling just making excuses. They made me angry, angry enough that the next day I jumped onto Tike's back and tried to ride him. Tike was so angry he dropped me off that cliff." I gasped, wondering how on earth my father had survived, Father chuckled then continued, "I think he would have been happy to let me fall he was so angry. He would have seen me die for the first few seconds of his rage then, as I flailed in the air crying and begging, he swooped down and saved me, I don't think he saved me for the moment

68

we'd just had he saved me for the days and months of good moments we'd had before. Then he flew away, far away and I never saw him again." The story was heartbreaking in a way, a tale of arrogance and peer pressure, force and insecurity, adolescent anger and deep love and caring. Father kept talking, his face the picture of despair and sadness. "That day I learnt one thing; the only thing Elves should ever ride is a horse, they are bonded to us. But Dragons and Griffins, Manticores and Phoenix's, they are free and wild spirits who would hate to be ridden by a stranger, as we would. Also, that story shows what can happen if you let your emotions take control. Be a monarch first and a person second. Rule first, live second and always be prepared to die for your kingdom."

# Scouting Out

The stars were stretched out across the bright sky, glinting and glowing. The Palace was silent as was the valley and the wood, Asir and I were dressed in loose black clothes with hoods so that we could blend better into the night. We did not even have our bows, just daggers, and weren't taking horses. Hako and Deon were sending us off. They both looked worried and fidgety, like they were trying to act confident.

"Remember to not engage unless they are about to kill you, act like you're invisible and you will surely become invisible." Deon instructed, I nodded and turned to Asir.

"Ready?" Asir nodded.

"Ready."

"Well then," I smiled, drawing my daggers and turning down the hill.

"Let's go."

We reached the camp quickly, stealing around the men on guard and slipping back to where the tents were. As we hid under a cart, we saw some of the Arial riders, they looked at ease, laughing together talking, like normal people. A soldier clearly in some position of authority rode over upon a Manticore. The man was tall and thin with dark hair and pale skin, his eyes were a watery blue, and his face was driven and square jawed. The men shuffled slightly into a state of mild attentiveness, saluting lazily.

"Captain!" The Captain yanked on his Manticore's reins and pulled it up short.

"Cleaves, where is your Cockatrice?" A young soldier not too much older than me scrambled to his feet and nodded to a large metal crate a few feet away. It would fit a Cockatrice, just, but the animal would not be able to move at all.

"In there Captain. Are they ready to clip him?" The Cleaves soldier asked. The Captain nodded. He clicked his fingers at an idle horse nearby and an elven slave seemed to detach from the shadows. The slave was almost skeletal, with pale skin and a shaggy mop of wild hair. He hitched the horse to the crate which showed to be wheeled and led it away.

"Are you going to trust him with a horse?" asked one of the soldiers. The Captain shrugged and frowned as if this hadn't occurred to him.

"Elf!" he shouted, the slave turned, his eyes were fearful, and his gaze seemed somehow broken. The Captain narrowed his eyes and said.

"If the Clippers don't have that Cockatrice in five minutes I will hold you entirely responsible and we will find you long before you can sneak back to whatever hell hole you crawled out of." The Slave nodded meekly and carried on walking.

The Captain engaged some more with the soldiers, but the small talk didn't seem to be getting us anywhere, so we left, peeping into tents and slipping into pens until we found a huge, gilded imperial looking tent. Asir and I crouched outside it, unsure as to what could be done. The doorway was guarded, and the guards were bristling with weapons and armour. Soon the figure of Casseil became apparent. He was walking on foot and did not appear the confident man of power he had seemed when we saw him at our court.

"Permission to see Phaeton please." He asked humbly, bowing his head. One of the Guards glared at him distastefully and the other slipped inside the tent. After a moment he returned with a grunt and nod. Asir pulled up the side of the tent and we wriggled under in the king's tent.

71

Phaeton's tent was huge, with the groundsheet lined with rugs and cushions of all colours. We crouched behind a large chest and peeped out over. Phaeton himself, or at least who we guessed was Phaeton, lounged on a deep red couch festooned with drapes and cushions. His body gleamed a shining dark brown and his eyes burned contrastingly blue. The same blue eyes that had shone out from beneath that hood. Phaeton was dressed for leisure, bare chested with a loose silken sheet of deep red wrapped around his legs. Dark braids covered his head, but stopped before his shoulders, clinging to the skin. On his fingers golden rings glittered and three small golden bands encircled his left ear. Phaeton waved a hand as Casseil stepped in.

"What news?" His voice was the one I'd heard earlier but was now rid of any intensity and only bore a lazy confidence. Casseil bowed.

"We're winning your majesty and..." Phaeton burst out laughing.

"Well of course we're winning Casseil. Honestly has living with this army for so long taught you nothing?" Casseil shifted uncertainly then continued.

"As you said, and our scouts confirm that they are scared and worried. It is predicted that we will have Charyass within the month." Phaeton glared at Casseil.

"We have the strongest and biggest army in the world. We have taken kingdoms twice the size of Charyass in a matter of days, and you mean to tell me that it will take a month to beat these plebs in armour." Casseil nodded meekly. Phaeton glared at him. For a split second he looked like he was about to leap upon Casseil and beat him, and by the way Casseil braced himself it was likely. But then Phaeton smiled. "Very well, what seems to be the obstruction?" Casseil nodded.

"Yes, this is the first kingdom who have called their creatures to help them, not at their command, as a request. So the beasts battle in the air and on the ground without a rider. It is strange." Casseil explained Phaeton nodded.

"I see. Will Malicious and I be needed?" Asir and I exchanged a look. Malicious sounded suspiciously like a dragon name. Dragons do not get named until they're fully grown; before that they have nicknames, pet names you might say. Casseil shrugged.

"I suppose it couldn't hurt. If you want this over soon anyway, they'd run screaming. But wait a while, I advise, maybe get the other ones out." Phaeton nodded.

"Good idea Casseil. I knew I kept you around for some reason, not just to be my manservant, though you aren't too bad at that. On that note would you like to see when my evening meal will be ready, and tell them if it's brought to me cold or if it's just a cold dish I will have them removed from the army." Casseil nodded,

"Yes sir." He walked out, though hugely muscular and powerful, under Phaeton's gaze he seemed small and flimsy; completely at Phaeton's beck and call.

We hurried out of the tent, wriggling from under the flaps and surveying the nighttime scene. Most of the soldiers were still up. The warm glow of the forge drew us to it. Inside, the Dwarves were sweating away, stripped to their loincloths as was usual when they were working. In the neighboring tent Dwarven women weaved and mended clothes and uniforms. The Dwarves have quite strong roles for each sex. I disapproved but I wasn't one to mess with another's culture. Young children sat in the female tent, the woman occasionally giving gentle reprimands or instructions. As we watched, one child of about four toddled up to a woman's loom.

"Auntie," the girl said in a lisping voice, "When is Mummy coming back?" The Aunt looked at another woman, their eyes both full of pitying sadness and she mustered a crying smile.

"Soon little one, but don't forget your Daddy will be here soon, then he's going to tell you exactly when your mother will be home." The child seemed satisfied and unsuspecting of the fate of her mother which had been made plain to the older children and other seamstresses. Asir and I left them too, slipping away shaking our heads to rid them of the heartbreaking innocence of the child.

We came to a pen like the ones used for the creatures. Inside this one chained to posts and slumped against them in sleep were elven archers, their bows and quivers lying in their laps. The pen was guarded but not too heavily. I guess they were confident the chains would hold them. Past the elven pen we found the place where that Cockatrice had been sent, the clippers. They were working on a Griffin when we arrived, clipping and cutting away the feathers on one of its wings, an operation that might be carried out on a chicken to stop them flying away, not a creature built for Arial life. Not a creature as majestic and lethal as the Griffin. They must have drugged it somehow as the Griffin was fast asleep. They were talking when we arrived, one big brutish looking man said, "Shame, this one's a fine specimen."

His friend laughed. I noticed the human soldiers had no women. I guess they shared the same gender barriers as the Dwarves, though Dwarven women were known for their prowess in battle.

"You know how it is, as soon as one turns vicious and tries to bolt in the air, we have them down on the ground." He gestured with his huge shear-like contraption. The first man nodded.

74

"Shame though, the Arials aren't doing too well, losing too many of these brutes." His friend nodded and wrinkled his nose drawing attention to the thick black ring he had pierced in it.

"Arials, they think they're so high and mighty just because they can sit on an animal with wings, upstart snobs I say." The other nodded, his head was shaved and tattooed with the image of a battle axe.

"I agree with you there," the one with a ring through his nose snorted, "and don't get me started on those guards, don't you think Aaric?" The one with the tattoo who I took to be Aaric gave a gruff chuckle.

"All they do is stand around all day and they think they can boss us around when we save so many of those blasted arials' lives by cutting these things, not to mention supplying the cavalry with some other steeds apart from those Centaur creeps. And those elf archers have an attitude. Did I tell you about what happened yesterday Nerian?" Nerian shook his head and the ring in his nose swayed slightly.

"Tell me all." Aaric seemed like he wanted to get this off his chest.

"One just told me I should be ashamed of both myself and my kingdom and that I should rethink the choices in my life. I naturally shut the impertinent little wretch down, wangled with one of their keepers and got it sentenced to solitary confinement for a while. It deserved it." The two laughed together, reveling in the gross objectivization of the elven archers.

"They're just as arrogant as Arials, Elves," Nerian spluttered as Asir and I slipped away, We didn't want to stay with them any longer.

Next, we came to the Centaur's pen. The centaurs were all awake, pacing and brooding. The walls of their pen were high, and their hooves were all weighted down making it harder to jump. Two were talking near the side of the fence we were crouched at. They were both female and identical, quite literally identical. I supposed they were twins. They both had long thick blonde hair and hazel eyes.

"Do you think we'll survive?" One was saying to the other.

"I hope we will. The people of Charyass aren't striking us, they know we're not at fault." This woman was softly spoken and her pitch was high, whereas her sister was more frightened and less thought through, her voice lower and more irrational in a way. When two people are so similar sometimes you must read into the tiniest little things to tell them apart. The one with the low voice spoke again.

"Yes, but they can't keep getting the rider not us, and what if they strike, Octavia, what if they kill." The one with the gentle voice, clearly Octavia, shrugged,

"I cannot say sister. I just hope it doesn't happen. Tell me, tell me how long it's been." The one with the low voice took her sister's hand.

"A year today, happy anniversary." Octavia laughed sadly.

"Happy Anniversary Abigail, and to the hope we will soon be free." Abigail nodded.

"I pray so sister for if not I fear that I will lose my mind."

My heart was pounding as was my head, simmering and seething with anger, these humans all needed punishment, and we had to win to free their slaves, we had to win. Asir touched my arm lightly and mouthed, "We should go now."

I agreed and we ran through the camp back into the dense wood. But we didn't head back to the elven camp. Instead I led him to a moonlit clearing. "Hey what's going on?" He was startled and frightened, but a slow smile was beginning to creep across his lips. I moved closer to him,

76

bringing my body up against his, his hands folded around my waist and his face came close to mine. Less than two or so inches taller than me it wasn't hard for us to kiss, in fact he barely had to bend down. His eyes were such a deep amber, like pools of tree sap, the lifeblood of a tree. Our lips connected. His were so cold and soft, startlingly cold, but mine soon warmed them. We were connected in that glade, still and dark like another tree, bound together, intertwined by our arms. But only when we slipped apart for a moment did I actually accept that I was in love. I was in love with Asir and I wasn't about to fight it.

"That was nice," I said flashing him a smile,

"Umm, yeah." Asir said, his eyes sparkling as we hurried back to the palace.

# Call Of The Dragons

I woke to a hammering at my door, Deon burst in a few seconds after I'd been roused, I didn't sleep for more than a few hours due to our late-night scouting mission turned kiss. Due to this I was also in particularly good spirits and looking forward to doing the same again some time.

"Hey Deon." I said amiably, I must have been smiling goofily because Deon frowned and snapped,

"Leaving aside whatever you must have done with Asir last night we have a problem." I frowned.

"One, you have absolutely no proof anything untoward took place last night and two, what's the problem?" Deon threw back my curtains. I could see the valley and the battlefield and hovering above the Human army were two huge Dragons.

"How big and what damage?" I asked as I joined my Father and Hako on the highest point.

"Fully Grown, and big ones too, they seem to be chained to the ground and are being shot with hot arrows to make them breath fire on our troops. They know if they hit the camp they'll be killed, so they have to hit us instead." Father replied, "They're causing a lot of damage, devastating our numbers faster than ever before, they're lethal." He continued, running a hand through his hair.

"Father thinks we only have one option," Hako added staring through a telescope,

"And that is?" I ventured. Father sighed,

"To get our own Dragons."

I was shocked. I didn't think Father would ever ask for the Dragon's help. He was too scared, but I supposed it was required for this situation. We needed Dragons to save us.

"I'll go," I said cheerily. I kept volunteering for these ventures because I found them more exciting than battle. The battle was exciting but to be honest it was a little too horrifying and heartbreaking for me to find any thrill. Father nodded at me smiling. "And I'll take Asir." I could sense Deon mouthing his objections behind me and gave one of legs a thump. Father shook his head.

"No, not after what happened last night," I groaned,

"Nobody has any proof of what happened last night." Hako raised an eyebrow.

"What did happen last night Athena?" I glared at him.

"We kissed if that's a crime now." Father seemed genuinely shocked. I rolled my eyes at him.

"It's not like he's the first boy I've ever kissed." Father frowned.

"Still if that's what you can do in one night, I am not leaving you together for what could be days. Hako can go instead." Hako's eyes were bright and his ears were twitching and flicking. He had never been allowed on a quest like this before.

"Can I father? Oh, thank you."

I chuckled at Hako's eagerness, but I was happy to have him along. It would be fun, even if I wished I could have Asir instead.

"You should leave right away. We can have your supplies ready in under an hour then you need to be off. The Dragons probably won't hurt you without good reason," Father explained. Then he pointed at Deon. "Deon you can't go, and neither can Tull. You'll both have to stay here. Don't worry, I'm sure my children will be fine." Deon looked like he was about to protest but he just bowed his head and turned with Tull.

"Let's get their things ready," Tull suggested, Deon nodded and the two trotted off. I smiled at Hako, enjoying his obvious merriment.

"We should get a move on; our troops won't last long without more reinforcements."

Hako and I both mounted. I on Luna, Hako on his chestnut horse called Maat. Hako had only had Maat for about a year. He'd got him on his fifteenth birthday, the same age I'd been when I got Storm. Oh Storm! I felt guilty, as my thoughts had completely skipped him recently. I felt hot tears spring burningly to my eyes. I missed him so much in my heart, I had a hole and unfortunately great as Luna was she could never replace him. Maat was a fine mount I guess, strong and powerful, but he didn't hold the same personality as Storm used to, or indeed Luna. Storm had been a great grandchild of my mother's mount Clover. And he had been so dedicated and loving to me. Anyway, I attempted to shut it out. I did not have time to be sad right now. I had to find the dragons and help Charyass win.

We were heading to the only proper mountain range in Charyass, known as the Vacrian mountains. Dragons lived most concentratedly there, namely we were heading for the highest peak that was where the most powerful Dragon lived. The Dragon Timeless had power over the other dragons and could call them to arms. Unfortunately, the mountains were a few days away at least. After the first day, Hako and I made camp atop a small hill. We'd only made small talk on the journey and only occasionally, but as we rolled up in our cloaks to sleep, Hako called out to me.

"Hey Athena."

"Yeah," I groaned sleepily.

"Do you think the dragons will come? I mean they can just fly to another kingdom, and if they stayed here, they would probably wouldn't be captured." I shrugged from within my cloak.

"We won't know until we get there." Hako nodded and then with his voice shaking asked.

"Will we be able to win the war without them?" I sighed deeply.

"I don't know Hako. I honestly don't know."

The next evening, we could see the mountain range as we bedded down by a river, a few adolescent merpeople flocked to the side of the bank when we arrived. We crouched down to talk to them prompting a few to heave themselves onto the bank, their tales shining.

"What brings you here?" asked a young mermaid with thick sable curls and bluish green eyes. Hako smiled at her,

"We're looking for the dragons, we must call them to the army." The girl looked at us again and her eyes widened.

"Oh, you're the Prince aren't you, and you must be," her eyes swiveled to me, "Princess Athena?" I nodded, laughing. The mermaid hastily attempted a bow though she was lying out on the bank, so it was hard.

"I was going to volunteer for the army you know, but I didn't know if it would work, how are the merpeople fighting anyway?" I was about to answer but Hako started before me.

"We're digging a channel for them; it won't be ready for a while I think but it will mean for a few days the land troops can rest and let the merpeople fight for a while. The mermaid nodded and flicked a wet strand of hair over her shoulder.

"Do you think I should volunteer? I'm rather good with a Trident." Hako shrugged.

"Maybe, I guess we need soldiers so yes volunteer and fight for your freedom." The mermaid nodded and was about to dive under when Hako called out to her, "Hey what's your name?" She turned and grinned.

"Kaia." Hako beamed.

"Well when I get back, I'll come visit your regiment."

"And you make fun of my whirlwind romances," I said as we lay by the crackling fire that night. Hako glared at me.

"Kaia is a valiant and brave soul who wants to fight for Charyass."

"So is Asir," I retorted, Hako gave an overly enthusiastic yawn right at me and replied.

"Well I wasn't flirting with her." I rolled my eyes at him,

"Oh, because saying you'll come visit her isn't flirting, I can tell when you turn on the charm brother, you like her." Hako rolled his eyes at me, he was getting almost as good as me at that, I guess I'd trained him well.

"Are we ten again? I am perfectly allowed to like whoever I want," I raised an eyebrow.

"And I'm not?" Hako nodded defiantly.

"You're the heir to the kingdom, you have to represent us." I glared at him.

"All the more reason to have a partner I love and trust." Hako shrugged.

"You could trust Tiberis."

"What is it with all you people and Tiberis? He was like some golden boy or something to you, what makes him so special huh?" I ranted. Hako looked at the floor. "What!" I shouted.

"Well he had a good family," Hako began,

"So does Asir his father was General Yan, rest in peace." Hako nodded.

"He also had a lot of money."

"We don't need money." I snapped. Hako nodded again humoring me.

"And I think Father liked him because he was so straightforward, easy to read you know, and that elf loved to grovel and flatter, he was more like your lap dog." I laughed at that.

"He was boring, that's why we broke up, he was so proper and polite, never wanted to do anything fun, not like Henck, now he was a fun boy." Hako chuckled.

"Wasn't he *too* fun?" I shook my head.

"No, I liked how fun he was. It was his wild recklessness I didn't love and anyway he was a merman and a sea one at that, it would never have worked." Hako shrugged.

"If you say so, anyway I'm clean I've only had one."

"Oh yeah what even happened to you and Lana, you were together for like a year." Hako looked at the ground. He was suddenly noticeably quiet. I got the sense he was hiding something. When they had broken up Hako hadn't talked for days and then he'd just acted as if it'd never happened. I frowned at him. "Come on now, tell your big sister what's up." When Hako looked at me his eyes were filled with tears.

"She was seeing a centaur while we were together, Lana swore it had only been for a week or two, but I didn't know, I left her right then and there." Rage filled me, pure throbbing rage. I'd always assumed they'd come to a mutual agreement, but Lana was cheating on Hako, on my baby brother. That wasn't something I'd stand for.

"Didn't you get her punished? Father could have sent her packing, or at least fired her. She's a maid for goodness sake. Why didn't you kick her out?" Hako shrugged.

"I wanted to, I really did, but I didn't want to tell Father what she'd done, it would be too humiliating." I got up from the ground and walked over to Hako wrapping my arms around him and holding him tight.

"I'll make her pay. Don't worry, I'll make her pay."

By midday the next day we had reached the mountains and on the highest peak got to the point where we could no longer use horses. We were shuffling along on our feet, Timeless's cave was all the way at the very top. Some said part of it led to the hollowed out core of the mountain and that Timeless would swoop around inside, though that was a legend that I'd never quite believed in. Dragons were entirely solitary though in times of need they would form a dignity, and that was a really magnificent sight, hundreds of dragons all flying together or hunting together. Very few had ever been seen and most who had seen it didn't live too long afterwards. We didn't talk at all on the journey but just climbed higher and higher though the air got increasingly thinner and it got a lot colder. We were grateful for our hooded fur lined cloaks.

Finally, though it was nearing evening we reached the cave. It seemed empty at first but as soon as we stepped inside there was a rumbling and a voice in our minds spoke loud and clear.

"Why have you disturbed me during my time of meditation?" We became aware of the huge grey head lying a few meters in front of us and then the two eyes snapped open the gaze focusing on us in a moment. Those eyes held all the history of the ages, everything that had ever taken place in the last few centuries, they were truly ancient and truly wise. The head raised on the long powerful neck and the leathery thick skin was hard and similar to the rock of the mountain. I inclined my head in respect and Hako did the same hurriedly.

"We apologise for the intrusion of your honor but I assure you our matter is of much urgency." Their eyes sparkled with amusement and we heard the voice in our heads again, slow and deliberate, deep and powerful.

"When is the trouble of mortals of any urgency, your lifetimes are so short and futile, what of any actual importance do you accomplish, will the world stop spinning? I doubt it, will the sun cease to shine? or the waves stop flowing?" I paused suddenly unsure of myself, then I continued carefully choosing my words.

"This matter could result in affecting Dragons greatly. You see a war is being fought at present between Charyass and a human army from an unknown Kingdom. This army have chained elves as archers, Centaurs as horses. Griffins and Cockatrices to ride into the air, all chained and bridled like livestock. And most importantly they have three Dragons, chained to the ground and being shot at with burning arrows to make them breath fire. We need your help, the other creatures have already weighed in to fight with us, for their freedom. The elven king sent us to you to beg, unashamedly beg for you to fight alongside us and so Charyass can win and put this army to a stop. Please Timeless, help us."

Timeless regarded us both with huge eyes, they were the colour of the sky on a clear day and so deep and full that you could stare into it for hours and always see a new thing. Dragon eyes aren't conventional colours, they can be any colour of the rainbow and even some that aren't in the rainbow.

"So, you want us to help you fix a petty little squabble over what exactly?" The Dragon sounded so bored and dismissive that I glared daggers at them.

"For your freedom you imperious know it all!" I screamed. Hako grabbed my arm and I stared at Timeless with my heart slowly icing over with fear as their eyes darkened from a clear sky to a thunderstorm, For a split second it was complete silence, the air was electric with tension and I stood unmoving. Then the Dragon rumbled low in their throat, laughter, I realized, deep loud Dragon laughter. Their voice came again in my mind.

"Oh, I haven't had any humanoids come visit me in a long while. I forgot how amusing you are when you get angry, especially young ones." I didn't like the patronizing tone, but I thought it better than being burned alive.

"So, your excellence?" asked Hako tentatively, "Will you help?" Timeless stared at us for a long while then their voice rang through our heads.

"You two are the king's children then?" We nodded. Timeless seemed to be growing thoughtful. His eyes seemed to be misting over like a thin layer of morning fog had covered the sky. "You did say that your opponents have three dragons?"

"Yes, Timeless we did," I said hurriedly. Timeless nodded slowly.

"Then I shall send you three dragons, make you even so that you can fight out the squabble between yourselves." There was a pause then Timeless's eyes cleared and glowed bluer and brighter than ever before they snorted and opened their mouth in a low far reaching bellow. Then they spoke again, resting their great head on the ground once more. "They'll be here soon, until then, please take a seat." He flicked a huge ear to the cave wall where what looked like they could be benches were carved into the rock.

"Do you get a lot of humanoid visitors then?" Hako asked as we sat. Timeless seemed to be resolved to the fact they would have to humor us, so replied.

"No, but I like to be prepared. The king on occasion comes to ask for advice, and a few young ones turn up every few years, usually in the form of a dare or such, proving their bravery. I have no time for shallow and arrogant children. They think they're so big and mighty just because they said hello to The Dragon Timeless, I tell them that of course." Hako nodded knowingly.

"Yes, being the Alpha must be tough, how often do you have to see other dragons?" Timeless's eyes glittered with a sort of amusement and near to what could have been liking.

"Every time a new Dragon comes of age, I must name them, and the adults meet every five years to discuss matters. And then there are the disputes over territory and such that people need my advice on." Just as they finished talking, we heard the flapping of wings and another Dragon head pushed through the cave entrance.

This Dragon was female with eyes of a deep murky purple and a shining black body. Timeless and her had a brief discussion on a mental wavelength that we couldn't tune into and then Timeless introduced us.

"This is Mystia, she is a strong fierce fighter and hunter." After Mystia came Majesty who turned out to be Mystia's twin with the same black skin but eyes of more of a violet. Majesty didn't pay us much heed. He just yawned, showing his fang filled mouth and greeted his sister. Finally, there was Silverhurst. A beautiful female silver dragon with gleaming skin and blue eyes that flowed like water. As we made ready to leave, I had a thought.

"As we need to be back as soon as possible I don't suppose you could fly us there, we wouldn't have to ride you or anything just let us hold onto a wing or something it would be much faster. All the dragons looked amused and Silverhurst nodded, snatching up both me and Hako with one talon by our cloaks. "Our horses too." I let out a strangled cry as we were yanked into the air and Silverhurst dived down the side of the mountain wings folded. Hanging by her claws, this was not fun, not fun at all. We stopped for a moment about halfway down for Mystia to grab Luna in one talon and Majesty to grab Maat with one too. Then we plummeted again, this time it was more exhilarating, and I was more at ease, because we had the dragons now and we had a chance at victory.

# Switching Things Up

When we were carried into the valley it was to huge applause. Though looking very undignified I still was able to revel in it. However, when Silverhurst playfully flicked me to Mystia who pretended to let me fall before snatching me out of the air I wasn't enjoying myself quite as much. Hako got a similar treatment, though they were more careful with our horses, gently setting them down. Leas ran out to meet us grinning up at the Dragons.

"Oh Brilliant, simply Brilliant, please return the Princess and Prince to their rightful places on the ground and then help to combat the other attack." Mystia hovered a few feet above the ground and dropped me. Majesty, who had ended up in possession of Hako after the game of catch, did the same. Then the Dragons turned and swooped away towards the battlefield. I looked around and noticed something strange.

"Hey Leas, why are so many soldiers here and not on the battlefield, and where are all the mer soldiers?" Leas pointed to where Father was standing on the highest peak.

"Come along Athena, you too Hako, we made some changes while you were gone."

The Battlefield had transformed, the middle of it had been dug into a huge lake of muddy water with Merpeople fighting. Phaeton's troops were wearing heavy collars that would slow down any fast water movements so they couldn't escape. Some non mer soldiers had waded into the water to fight as well but they weren't doing as well.

"What is happening Father?" I asked, Hako and I joined him. Father kissed both of our heads and for a moment hugged us close before replying.

"Dragons can't burn water, and the merpeople need to fight. The Phoenixes have been keeping the Dragons at bay due to the fact they are fireproof. But they are far smaller than the Dragons and are no real match for them even if they can breathe fire." I nodded watching the merpeople. Our mer soldiers were drowning the human troops and trying to pull the collars off the mer slaves, so they could escape. The land faring soldiers weren't doing too well, but they were surviving. The three Dragons we'd brought sailed up towards the enslaved ones and began clawing and tussling together.

"This will buy us some time, but even Dragons won't save us, we need a miracle," Leas's words were grave as we watched, Father nodded slowly then forced a smile.

"Why don't you two children go get some rest, you can jump onto the battlefield in the morning."

As I walked towards my hut, I ran into Asir. He looked surprised to see me.

"Hey, your back already," he said slowly. I nodded.

"Yeah, anything interesting happened when I was gone?" Asir shrugged.

"They dug a big pit and put water in it." I peered out at the aquatic battlefield and nodded.

"You're really the expert of perception today aren't you." Asir laughed, then carried on walking.

"Thalia wants another report on our scouting mission, you need to come you left before she could ask you." I nodded and was about to walk when I shivered and looked down at my three-day old armour clothes and cloak.

"Wait, Asir you go on ahead I'll change then catch you up." Asir shrugged and nodded.

"See you later then," I smiled.

"Yes, see you."

Deon was as usual standing outside my chamber, and he looked relieved to see me.

"You survived and succeeded," he shouted as if it was the best and most shocking thing ever.

"Yes," was my reply as Deon gave me a little hug and then ushered me into my room. I put on some loose green cloth trousers and a long coat that brushed past my knees. Then I hurried out to give Thalia the full report. I would have to say that I was glad to be back, it hadn't been too enjoyable being away when I knew they were in such danger, and I'd missed everyone, especially Asir, though I hadn't thought of him now I saw him again I realized I had missed him. I'd also worried for my Father, and Leas and Deon and everyone else, I was glad to be home.

"So, tell me again, these 'clippers' what exactly were they doing?" Thalia asked again, the young scribe next to her was still vigorously writing and Thalia's pencil was poised over her paper ready for more drawing.

"They were clipping the wings of the flying animals that weren't obeying them so they couldn't fly anymore and so they could use them for the cavalry instead." Thalia nodded and clicked her fingers at the elven girl scribing.

"You get all that Liyoni?" The girl nodded though her hand was still moving at unnatural speed. Thalia smiled. "This is Liyoni my apprentice, she can write so fast I have her make notes, and I'm helping train her in completely replicating drawing so she can be a scout and sketch artist like me." Liyoni nodded.

"Yes, this is my first week, I'm having a great time." Liyoni's voice was soft and rich, sweetly soothing too, it was a highly recognizable voice, that was the only recognizable thing about her. Liyoni seemed to blend, like a lot of wood elves her hair was the exact shade of tree bark and her eyes were a pretty but generic hazel. She was of average height and had that kind of familiar, forgettable face, even featured, heart shaped, coupled with long sharply pointed ears that didn't flick or twitch very much.

"Pleased to meet you," I said and Asir nodded.

"You are in the training for an honorable occupation," Liyoni smiled shyly and nodded.

"Yeah, that's why I chose it, I was so lucky to have Thalia as my mentor and trainer though." Asir nodded,

"How old are you?" He asked, frowning, Liyoni seemed a little old to be just starting off as an apprentice. For trades such as tailor and Blacksmith, productive ones that required quite a lot of training you would begin at around fourteen or fifteen. If you were to clean or serve you would start older as the jobs were more straightforward. For the army you could begin training at sixteen, but you wouldn't be able to fight till eighteen. Unless of Course you were Hako, because Hako is a prince. I was not sure how being a scout's apprentice worked, but Liyoni seemed about my age.

"Oh I'm eighteen I've just finished my two years of military training before I can start," This was an interesting way of doing things and I mulled over it slowly while Asir went through the entire conversation we'd overhead Nerian and Aaric saying.

"Athena, could you please describe these two to me?" Thalia asked, I nodded hurriedly.

"Yes, they were both tall and big, muscular I mean, sort of thuggish in a way, one, Nerian had a ring pierced through his nose and the other Aaric had a shaved head with a battle axe tattooed upon it. Nerian had dark hair I think but their faces were turned partly away from us, so it was hard to work out their features." Thalia's hand moved across the page in a frenzy similar to how Liyoni wrote, with long deft strokes she soon shaped two men with their backs to us, one with a tattooed scalp and another who was only half turned so we could just about see the ring through his nose.

92

"That's brilliant," Breathed Liyoni from behind us. I turned to her.

"If you're half as good as that, you're ready for a job." I said smiling. "Come on what can you do, I'm okay at drawing, but I prefer to write, it's far easier, anyway come on draw a dragon." Liyoni shyly stepped back shaking her head but Thalia wagged a finger.

"No, this is good for your confidence. Liyoni, draw a dragon." Then, addressing me and Asir, with an impressed smile, "She's amazing really, better than I was at her age by far." Liyoni took a piece of blank paper and began with light strokes of her charcoal to shape a Dragon. Soon it was done and looking closely I saw she had drawn Mystia, the resemblance was uncanny for a drawing. It held the same aloof grace and elegance, coupled with such power and supernatural strength. The skin was colored black with the charcoal pencil and the eyes were uncolored but anyone who had once seen Mystia would be able to fill in the dark purple that the eyes were. The image however didn't so much depict a dragon who looked like Mystia as a very specific dragon called Mystia and something about the pose she was in, her wings outstretched and her head turned towards us seemed a lot more like a picture than a sketched image. Like she was an artist rather than a scout. I loved the picture, snatching it up to look more closely. I smiled then turned to Liyoni.

"If you do this again as a painting I will pay you for it, handsomely, we have the materials at the palace, just ask a servant to show you some of the artists' chambers, they are filled with that stuff." Liyoni looked at Thalia beseechingly and Thalia nodded with shrug.

"Some extra money for your family can't hurt, and I don't have any more tasks for a few days, you'll be free to work on it." Liyoni nodded gratefully and smiled at me,

"Thank you Princess, I will do all I can." Her lilting tones furthered to lull and soothe me.

"Well tell me when it's finished, I've got to get going, Deon's outside, see you later."

Deon was waiting for me his eyebrows raised as I came closer to him.

"Been in there a while haven't you, I nodded,

"Yeah. Thalia has a new apprentice, Liyoni, she's amazing, she's painting me a picture." Deon nodded as his hand whirled around my shoulder, I could see out of the corner of my eye his fingers gesturing Asir away as his arm wrapped around me.

"Glad to have you back Princess, I missed you a great deal you know, and with all the changes being made to the army I couldn't bear to just let you go out. I almost went after you." I laughed.

"You take body guarding too seriously Deon." Deon shrugged but continued to march me if subtly back to my chambers.

# More Chilling Tales

The knock on my door wasn't one that was familiar to me, it was not Deon's as it had no abrupt but respectful request to it, or Hako's as it lacked the fearful gentleness. Melissa scarcely ever knocked, usually getting Deon to do it for her and when she did it so tentatively, I could barely hear. The knock lacked the authority I would equate with Father's or eagerness Asir had posed the few times he'd knocked on my door. It did however bare a familiarity nagging away at my subconscious, trying to unearth a memory.

"Come in," I called, replacing my quill upon the table and standing up from my parchment. Leas entered and stared at my careful inked words, I remembered his knock now from when I was a child the soft but expecting tones now becoming clear to me and I filed it away in my mind.

"You seem to be writing a letter, though I am unaware as to whom it may concern." I frowned as Leas lifted the page, "This battle is not proceeding with a promising outcome; on the contrary even with three dragons the sheer might and immorality of this army seem to be close to crushing us within the month, this is what they believe anyhow." I glared at him; this was the first time Leas had ever made me angry.

"That's for Timeless," I snapped, Leas frowned at me uncomprehending, "They asked to be kept abreast of the developments, I'll send it to him via a dove later. Leas frowned and then shrugged, replacing the page on the desk.

"I came to comfort you, after the journey your father thought you may need some normalcy," he tossed me a heavy satchel. Opening it, I found it was crammed full of old books. Ones of ancient proportion, with worn and tattered covers and elaborately inked golden titles. They were tales of adventure by the looks of them, but others were more factual. Some covered highly relevant straightforward topics such as foraging, but others covered more philosophical subjects such as the Art of war. And One which Leas was pleased to see I focused on bore an intricate title is sparkling gold contrasting with the hard-aged black cover. I stared down at it, drinking in the title which read:

**Catalogue of The Ancient Ones**

I stared down at it, enchanted by the elaborate swirl and curl of the letters. Leas looked down at it fondly.

"That book was a gift to me from my father when I was a child, I loved it, it has drawings and great detail about all the Ancient creatures that once populated our world, some are definitely no more, and others most probably pure creatures of myth but it is still a great read, and if some of the ancient ones are still around it might tell of where they live. The old Satyr sat beside me with a heavy sigh and opened the book. On the first page a huge Leviathan snarled out at me, the jaws agape, the saliva dripping from them slowly.

Leas let me flick through the pages for a minute before confiding, "Athena I worked out where these people come from." I jumped and looked up easily.

"Really, how?" Leas gestured to my covers and waited for me to get settled underneath then began.

"Don't think it was easy, I had to consult the Council of The Learned, and pour over endless maps and books." Leas was referring to a council filled with ancient scientists and philosophers who pretty much knew everything, Leas was a member. "Luckily some of my more travelled colleagues had some scraps of rumors, mainly the tales of old drunken sailors, but I found some really ancient maps that tell of the other side of the world, far far away and I came across a country known as Barrow, Barrow has few humanoid fantastic creatures. Humans are the dominant species. Then I found a scroll telling of the event that happened several years ago leading to The March Of The Barrownians. So the scroll tells that the old king of Barrow, Keerian, was his name, had two children, Phaeton and Mira. The humans are terribly sexist it seems only men can do anything of note such as have power or fight. So, Phaeton had to inherit the throne. Upon the death of their mother Phaeton ran away from the palace and spent a year alone in which he bonded with a creature, then when Phaeton heard of his father's sickness he returned and was soon crowned king. Soon after Phaeton was king, invading armies came to Barrow, Phaeton's army destroyed these in days and then with his heart and mind alight with the thrill of war he continued to fight, marching through the kingdoms and enslaving all they passed." I stared at Leas slowly comprehending the thought of a wild and mad young Phaeton in his first few months of king marching for world domination.

I lay in bed with Leas thinking and me pondering for a few more minutes before Leas said,
"How about a myth, to send you to sleep, like we did when you were a child." I laughed and smiled up at him lying down on my bed.
"Which one?" I asked. Leas sighed,
"What about the one about Athena, you know the elf girl you were named after." I smiled fondly.
"Mother always loved that one, there was a song about it she used to sing me at night," Leas nodded.
"Well are you ready?" I nodded. "Then I'll begin."

"Many years ago, when the world was still wild and treacherous, full of warring tribes and creatures so viscous you couldn't imagine them, when magic was still commonplace. There was a tribe, they were known as the Sage tribe and their Chief was a strong and peaceful man, but he fell victim to the most vicious of tempers. He had a daughter, Athena, who was the most precious thing to him in the world, he loved her so much and all the other tribes knew that. For that reason, Athena had a lot of protection. But one day Athena was in the woods with a bodyguard, she was climbing a tree when a man pounced on her bodyguard who was a Centaur, the elf, who attacked killed the centaur in seconds with the element of surprise and then more elves came and they surrounded Athena's tree and took her. These Elves were part of the Charki tribe which wanted some of the Sage territory. Athena knew that her father would go mad when he found out, he'd be at war with the Charki's in moments but she also knew that this would crush the tribes which had lived in harmony for so many years close together. She knew a war would result in one of the two incredibly powerful tribes leaving the territories. And wipe out a major trade source for the other. Athena was sitting in the hollowed out wooden tree trunk they kept her in and deliberating what she could do, there was really little that could be done and she was going to give up and let her father come for her but then she saw a sharp old rock in her cell and she began to chip and shave away the wood of the thick trunk. It took her two days before she had a hole to get out of, she graduated to a spoon when they brought her one to eat her food with. When Athena got out, she had to face the guards. Luckily, they were more expecting an attempt to rescue her, not an attempt to escape. Athena climbed through the tree canopy when she left, jumping between the branches. Then she arrived back at her village just as the army was about to attack. This war was averted, and Athena caused the rival territories to continue their peace."

By the end of the story I was pretty much asleep and Leas gently left, I thought of the song about Athena, it was truly quite bad tribal melody that Hako and I would heartily join in with when my mother sung it and if Father was around he would do so too I still remembered her merry lively voice being thickened by my father's base tones.

*Digging, digging, for peace for peace*
*Athena never gave up*
*She dug, she dug, she chipped away*
*Until the wood was gone.*

*Then she hid from the guards*
*And swung through the trees*
*For peace, for peace,*

*The Tribes were at war,*
*They needed her help*
*She saved them*
*For peace, for peace*

*Kidnapped, she thought*
*Imprisoned, she escaped*
*Alone, she ran away*
*And returned to her tribe.*

*War didn't happen*
*There was peace, there was peace,*
*Athena, Athena*
*She brought peace*
*She brought peace*
*Athena*
*Brought Peace*

# Malicious Arrives

I was back on the front line the next day battling it out on Luna. We pushed forward moving around the huge lake of water, so we stayed, shifting away from the merpeople. I thought of the other people around me, falling constantly, the death toll spiraling out of control. As I looked up high at the sky that was no longer clear. Filled with fire and feathers, screeches and fights of the creatures above. I missed peace, I missed it so much. I missed being able to look out on the serene valley. I missed being able to see the creatures free and wild. Now it was just a ravaged battle ground, full of blood, mud, water and tears. As I looked up, I saw a huge looming shape soar above. It was a huge battle-scarred dragon, fully grown, and massive. Larger than any of the five dragons already on the field. Its skin was jet black but marbled with veins of bright red like an active volcano. Fire spewed from its mouth and its huge wings beat steadily. Then as I looked up further, I saw a figure standing on its back. A figure in bright shining battle armour with a crimson cape attached to their shoulders. A figure with short braids on their head and dark skin. And most of all a figure with bright shining blue eyes I could make out even from this distance. Phaeton was riding a Dragon.

The three dragons on our side all flapped back in submission, the chains on the enslaved dragons were cut giving them complete freedom but instead of running they flanked Phaeton's dragon. The entire battlefield was transfixed by this site, they all stared up, not fighting. But the Barrowian army soon got over their initial shock and began to battle through their opponents, they were clearly used to this. I guessed this must be the creature Phaeton had bonded with, the animal Phaeton had referred to as Malicious when he was talking to Casseil. Fire swept over the troops, hoods were set alight, our troops screamed and ran in disarray, about the battlefield. My Regiment were turning to retreat, and I couldn't agree more but I attempted to maintain order.

"Lines form, fall back!" I yelled out to them, galloping Luna to the front of the retreating line away from the terror and carnage of Malicious.

"What was that!" I yelled as I marched into the war council that evening, barely noticing the glares of the others at my lack of decorum.

"We believe it to be a dragon who faced the same trauma and sadness Phaeton did when he was young and moping after his mother's death." Macos informed me with a steely glare. I smiled.

"Well he's unstoppable on that thing. He can control it exactly and the Dragon controls the other two. His name is Malicious, when I was scouting Phaeton mentioned him to Casseil." I informed the council. They nodded in interest and then Father said, "I don't know how we're going to fix this Athena." As I looked at him a slow idea began to form, gradually solidifying in my mind.

"I know what we might be able to do, we just need an elf to ride a different dragon." Macos gave me such a condescending look that I almost slapped him.

"What dragon would possibly do that; they take their pride very seriously." Macos sneered at me. I glared at him,

"A Dragon who had bonded with a human for a while." I looked at Father whose eyes widened in understanding and glared at me.

"No! Athena what do you think you're doing, that won't work." I shrugged.

101

"If it doesn't, we'll already be with Timeless for him to give us some advice." Father stared at me, for a long time before somehow relenting.

"Well we don't have anything better on the table." I was enjoying how infuriated Macos was becoming by not knowing what was going on.

"My king I must ask what you are talking about." Father gave Macos a weary glare.

"Macos, we're talking about Tike."

I waved Silverhurst down easily, she flicked her tail at our bags and cloaks and her thoughts were clear.

"Going somewhere?" I nodded, Father stepped forward,

"Silverhurst I would be honored if you would do Athena and I the favor of flying us to The Dragon Timeless, I can't leave the kingdom for long enough to make the journey by land, with you carrying me it would take a matter of hours." Silverhurst cocked her head to one side, then she gave the snarling figure of Malicious a sidelong look before grabbing me with one huge taloned paw and my father with the other.

"Get ready you two," her thoughts said, "I always fly my fastest."

Silverhurst hadn't been lying, she placed us down no more than two hours after we'd left, and it hadn't been a great experience. Silverhurst powered on constantly faster and faster until I was feeling sick and Father looked positively shaken. Timeless raised their head to see us.

"The king?" They sounded incredulous and pleased at Father's bow of respect.

"Yes, your majesty, I have a great favor to ask of you one I dare say I shall never be able to repay." Timeless looked extremely interested now.

"What is it?" They asked, I knew they could probably take a look through Father's mind, but they seemed to have respect for Father, one ruler to another it seemed.

"Well, Phaeton is riding a dragon he bonded with years ago and the only way we could combat this is by riding a different dragon, so I was wondering if you could summon an old Dragon I used to be friends with before we had a falling out, I don't know his name but I used to call him Tike." Timeless thought for a moment and it was amazing he opened his mind to us to the extent that we could hear all his thoughts and, in our mind's eye see all the images that flashed before him.

"I'll send out a signal, whoever this is will hear it and come." Timeless informed us before being completely silent for a moment and then lying their head back down again.

"Now we wait."

We waited for a while, and I could tell Father was nervous, after a while we heard wing flaps nearby and then a flame colored head thrust itself through the cave entrance. Father jumped up and stepped back, tears began to slowly stream from his eyes. The Dragon that must have been Tike had eyes that seemed so understanding, and intelligent. They were deep murky blue indigo, huge and staring. They were the colour of a stormy sea in the daytime. A colour that made you think you were falling in the swirling inky depths. They were the colour of the night sky shining and bedecked with sudden points of star like light. The colour of spilled ink flying across a page. That colour seemed to be everything and nothing, anywhere and nowhere, it seemed so familiar and so alien, like a buried myth that we all had dormant inside us.

"Tike?" Father whispered, the Dragon nodded slowly, and his words were so clear and glowing in my mind and held such knowingness and somehow love.

"Hello Kallias."

Nobody had called my father his name in years, and I hadn't heard it spoken since my mother was alive.

"What do you go by now?" Father asked, replied easily enough.

"Valiance, that's my name, I know what you want Kallias, I can still read your mind," Father dropped to his knees and bowed his head.

"Valiance, I am so sorry. I am so wrong and so pained by what happened. We were both young, we were both impulsive, but you, you were kind, graceful and loving. You could of let me fall and I would have held nothing against you if you had done so, but you didn't, and you saved me. You have the purest of hearts and if you're disgusted by my begging, you have every right to be. But I need your help Valiance, please, for your fellow creatures and dragons. I need you to let me ride you. I beg you to, I beg you entirely. Please Valiance, please." Valiance looked at my father for a moment, taking him in.

"You've grown Kallias, you've become a king and a man in what seems like moments." Father nodded. Valiance's eyes began to glow as if he were searching for something inside Father, this was a phenomenon I'd been taught about when a dragon can search through someone's soul. By just looking at Father, Valiance was deciding what to do. "When we were both young you used to come see me without your friends." Valiance said, "But I knew all about them, I watched you play with them, I watched you meet them. I looked out for you from a safe distance. You were Prince Kallias, none could touch you, but you never let that cloud your mind, that was why I was surprised when you tried to mount me." Father's head drooped some more. I had never seen him in this state of humility and humbleness, Valiance continued. His eyes were focused on Father staring at him, "But Kallias, after you mounted me and I threw you, as I watched you fall, I was struck with realization of your youth and fragility, of the human way of influence and tribalism. That is why I saved you, I knew you needed to learn, and you have learnt, and Charyass needs help. I will help!" Valiance let loose an almighty roar that shook the cave itself, a battle cry, so bright and shaking that I stumbled under the barrage of noise. But Father leapt to his feet and threw his arms around the Dragon's neck.

"It's been too long, my friend." He said, Valiance nodded.

"Far too long."

# End Of the First Chapter

Father flew back on Valiance's back, Silverhurst held me and I was envious of Fathers far more leisurely and comfortable ride. When we touched down everybody stared, Father elegantly stepped off Valiance's back and threw off his cloak.

"I'll go out now and fight." He said kissing me lightly on the forehead, "I trust you'll be down below." A servant handed Father his bow and quiver and another his daggers.

"Yes of course Father." I whistled for Luna who was brought to me instantly and I mounted her. Father jumped back on Valiance with a whoop of war and as Luna began to gallop Valiance soared into the air. His shadow darkening the area in which Luna ran, we zoomed in unison towards the battlefield.

Few of our soldiers were left out there, they were hanging back and cowering. But the Barrowian army was waiting. I fell against them in moments. Stabbing and cutting, kicking and slashing, my arrows flying into hearts and pinning soldiers to the ground. Luna showed no fear once again and neither did I. For I felt the shadow of Valiance over me and I felt unstoppable. I cast my gaze upwards and saw Malicious wheel around to face Valiance. With snarls and plumes of fire the two dragons crashed together, Clawing and snarling at each other. Phaeton and my father engaged too, their daggers and swords glinting with the sun's rays. A battle of the kings themselves. The two Dragons broke away for a moment an arrow zoomed through the air from Father's bow to Malicious side. The arrow seemed to have absolutely no affect. It was a blade so small and insignificant to a creature of such epic proportions. I was aware of a horse galloping beside me and I turned to see Deon.

"Be careful princess," he said through gritted teeth. Then I heard more hooves and saw Maat with Hako on his back, and behind Asir riding a huge dark horse. Asir shot me a rueful smile and our small four-man army battled against the increasing force of the humans and their creatures.

Up above, Phaeton yanked the arrow from Malicious' side and snapped it, tossing it aside as if it were nothing. Another zinged forward but Phaeton caught it in midair spitting down on the ground below in disgust. Father was angry now and so was Valiance, they swooped in close enough for Father to slash a wound in Malicious leg. The blood flow was minimal, and the animal showed little pain though the angry red eyes just bulged more. Malicious's wings were war torn and tattered at the tips, and his body was so scared that he must of gone through so much pain in his life, But it had made him a hard ruthless monster he was clearly his name through and through. From the glitter in his fiery eyes you could tell he was truly Malicious. And yet Phaeton controlled him with ease, they seemed united and together as one a joint force of angry strength. Communicating telepathically as they fought against Father and Valiance.

As I watched, Father shot three arrows at once. Two lodged in Malicious's neck, harmless but still causing the Dragon to flinch in pain. And the third sailed straight into his eye with the careful precision my Father always shot with. Malicious let out a guttural bellow of complete pain, writhing in the air as his eyes wept tears and blood. Taking advantage of this weakness, Valiance flew right up to Malicious and slashed at his chest and stomach clawing them open. The blood fell in heavy red drops onto the

107

soldiers, as they stared up at the fight. Malicious roared and snarled in pain but his wings began to fail, and the animal began to plummet downwards. Phaeton leapt from his dragon's back and a griffin flew up from the Barrowian ranks and caught the plummeting leader. I caught sight of Casseil on the animal's back. There were cheers from our side as the enemy scattered to make room for the huge body of Malicious that thudded into the ground. Valiance did a victory somersault with Father laughing on his back. Relief flooded me; we were free.

But then I saw the steadily approaching Griffin. Casseil must have been left on the ground because only Phaeton was there now. Phaeton was gripping a lance that must have been Casseil's as he didn't seem accustomed to it. Father didn't seem to see him yet, I screamed up at him.

"Father, look at the Griffin!" Valiance and Father turned as one dodging away, but too late. I watched with my heart steadily falling deep into my stomach as Phaeton with his mouth wide in a cruel triumphant grin ran his lance through my father's heart.

I watched him fall from Valiance's back. Slip off and tumble downwards, Valiance slashed the Griffin away like it was an annoying bird and swooped down after him. Phaeton flapped off astride his beast. Valiance folded in his wings and dived so swiftly he was merely a blur. Stooping and catching father in a wing so as not to show the body too much. Valiance brought him in from the battlefield toward the palace. I whirled Luna around and galloped on after. Praying that I'd seen it wrong, praying it was just a flesh wound. I fought back tears, I just urged Luna on, keeping her going faster and faster. I wanted to be there with him, to help him get better, because he had to survive this, for his kingdom, for himself, for me, my Father had to get through this.

He was gently laid out on a soft bed of springy grass when I arrived, his eyes bright and open, staring up at me. I tried not to look at the reddened bandage that swathed his chest. I averted my eyes from the bloodied lance lying beside him and I tried not to notice how pained he looked. Hako was beside me and shaking hard. I didn't realize I was crying until the bright clear tears splashed onto his face, shining golden in the setting sunlight. Father looked up at me and a weak smile played across his lips.

"You and your mother always look your most beautiful at two times," he said, "When you're crying and when you're in battle." I smiled as he looked past me at Hako, "My son." His voice was breaking, and he lightly touched his hand. I suddenly realized that Hako and Father had never done much together, Father had focused on me generally, it was me who had frequent meetings with him, me who had a seat on the council. But then I supposed Father had thought he'd be around for a while yet; he'd presumed he would be able to spend time with Hako when I was older. We'd presumed a lot of things. Hako clutched Father's other hand as I already held one.

"Father," he replied his voice breathy and scared.

"Athena will need your help; no monarch should reign alone. Your mother was my support, then Athena, you will have to be your sister's." Hako nodded.

"Yes Father of course." Tears were streaming down his grimy face, tracing lines of clean brown through the greyish brown muck.

"And Athena, you will have to be queen, very young, be strong and be brave, and on account of that elven boy." Father managed to wink at me.

"Yes?" I asked, wanting to hear what he had to say. Father sighed deeply.

"He and all the others you'll meet have my blessing." I smiled at Father despite all that was happening. "I fear I have little time left," He coughed for a short while, blood spewing in his spittle. He clutched our hands tighter.

"What is it Father?" Hako asked, he inclined his head in respect and we waited. Then King Kallias Of Charyass, my father, sighed deeply and leaned forward to us. He breathed in and in one strained whisper gasped,

"Find the ancient ones."

# The Aftermath

I watched as the life slowly drained from my Father's eyes, I watched his body go limp and rigid and Hako fall against me in tears. My own tears would not stop, they just flowed down my face into a river of briny water. Valiance appeared with his huge head staring at Father's body. It is an extremely rare occurrence to see a dragon cry, but I watched it happen. The tears spilled from his eyes glowing in the growing darkness as Valiance wept. Then he sent out such an epic telepathic pulse that the entire valley stopped what they were doing and gasped in sadness. Fresh tears pricked my eyes and I heard startled cries of sadness from every living thing in hearing range, and I knew the pulse had reached the entire kingdom. I was certain. Valiance roared in such a way you could feel his heart wrenching lament. His grief and his blame. He blamed himself so much. The tears of a dragon are powerful and sacred. They fell onto Father's body and glistened on him. They cleaned away the blood and the dirt until he lay there tidy and washed. Valiance then turned and launched high into the sky his fading telepathic message ringing in my ears.

"I cannot fight without Kallias. Goodbye."

I don't remember going to bed or changing from my armour. I don't remember the rest of that fateful evening, but I woke in my night dress with Hako curled up beside me. The pillows and sheets were both wet with our tears. Three people were waiting at the foot of my bed, Deon, Leas and Melissa, Deon bowed to me, as did the others, proper low bows of great respect.

"Good morning, my queen." Deon said, my eyes widened. I was queen now. I was queen of Charyass. I had to rule. I had to win this war. More tears seemed ready, but I held them back. I had to be strong. I had to be a queen. Leas embraced me in a hug, and I hugged back fiercely,

"I'm queen," I gasped as he let me loose. Deon nodded and Melissa bowed again.

"Queen Athena of Charyass." I stared at Melissa and then saw what was in her hands. A circlet of gold, my crown! It was not an eccentric thing, the Elven crowns aren't. No jewels or anything. Just a plain circlet of gold with a small peak for monarch and silver for Princes or Princesses. I gently woke Hako who yawned and snapped,

"What am I doing in your bed?" I smiled sadly.

"You shouldn't speak like that to your queen." Hako's shoulders slumped as the last day's events came flooding back to him. I saw the way his face fell, and his eyes brimmed with fresh tears.

"So, you're the queen now?" He asked again, unable to comprehend the thought.

"I'm afraid so." I replied.

"And Father's... Father is really gone?" I couldn't bring myself to answer that. But Leas did it for me.

"I'm afraid yes, his cremation is today, and you must attend, it is in a matter of hours, Hako, please Tull is outside he will lead you to your Chambers." Hako nodded sleepily and stood up, I laughed in spite of myself, for Hako was only wearing his underwear. Hako reddened and accepted the proffered cloak from a blushing Melissa. "Thank you," he said, wrapping it round himself in as dignified a way as can be possible in the situation. Then he walked out of the door.

Now I was left with the three people who'd raised me most aside from my parents. I felt like a scared little child, totally inadequate to rule without my Father there. If I'd felt sadness at losing Storm this was utter devastation, and horror and shock. I now had to try and win this war without my Father to help. "What am I going to do?" I asked them. Deon touched me lightly, "You're going to be the strong brave girl your Father knew you always were, Now come along let's get you ready."

And like so many days before I let Melissa draw me a bath. Like so often before I had my hair brushed and combed through, then let to hang in a loose sheet of wavy blonde. A dress was picked out for me, it was long and black reaching over my entire body. Large and flowing with a lot of fabric, different to my usual simple style. Unlike all the other times though this was done in almost complete silence and unlike every other time, I didn't have to rush, I didn't have to do anything because for the first time in my life I was in complete control, I could do anything, I was queen but also for the first time in my life I felt and cared about the pressure. When I was merely a Princess, I wouldn't care what people thought, but now I had to, they were my people, my subjects and I had to do the right thing. I had to win this war because they were entirely my responsibility. Also, what hit me was loss, the loss of both my parents, my orphaning, I had never felt so alone and so isolated. Everyone around me looked weary. Leas looked like he had aged just from seeing my sadness. Deon's eyes were ringed with dark circles and Melissa's face tired as she attempted to muster a worn smile once I was ready, "As usual queen," she said with a curtsy, "You look Divine."

The walk through the palace was something else. Everyone I passed bowed or curtseyed, they all mumbled a, "My queen," or a, "Your majesty," or even a, "Your highness." Deon trotted behind me importantly and glared at pretty much everyone. When I was just princess Athena the most I would get would be a head incline or a hurried,

113

"Princess," of acknowledgment. Now they all paid me optimum respect. I could no longer be free and rebellious, I now had to be a queen. I passed Asir, he bowed to me and said, "I'm sorry for your loss your Majesty," I gave him a pained smile, "Walk with me, I'm on my way to his burning, I wish you would attend." Asir looked so honoured and he fell into step with me easily. "So, Your queen now? Does that mean I can no longer court you?" I laughed slightly, though no laughter felt genuine, "Of course you can still court me, in fact my father gave you his blessing in his dying words." Asir's eyes widened, "Really? I feel so honoured, he was a true and noble monarch." I nodded, trying not to let on how much my heart was aching, how much I was crying deep inside.

So many people watched the body burn on the funeral pier, we all gazed on as the flames devoured the body, licking the ceremonial gold robe that Father wore. I gazed at Hako with my arm around his shoulder. I had to look like a queen even now, my crown was on, I stood straight, and I didn't weep. I didn't weep at all. I saw Macos standing nearby mourning and I made a note to get rid of him as soon as we composed ourselves as a working country. If we composed ourselves before Phaeton's army overpowered us.

Hako tracked me down afterwards, I was looking out at the battlefield from the highest point, the wind blowing my hair and dress and my eyes trained on the scene. A truce had been called as Phaeton had wanted to give Malicious a proper funeral and we had wanted to do the same with our king. But the remnants of war still lay, the stagnant pool of water, the blood, mud and trampled earth. The weapons strewn and dented across the field. It was a complete mess and I felt just like it. I felt like a battlefield with nobody fighting. Not being used yet carrying so much symbolism, I had made not one decision as queen yet, but I was queen, I was an eighteen-year-old queen of Charyass. "Hey," Hako said hesitantly. I turned and opened my arms to my little brother. His cheeks were wet and I held him close. "I miss him Athena," he said his voice trembling. "I know I didn't spend much time with him but I miss his presence, I miss him being there to watch over us." I knew exactly how Hako felt, I missed him so much, I missed everything about him. "I know," was all I could say, because I had to be a strong queen. I had to be a queen who would lead Charyass to victory.

I stood there with Hako for a long while, mind flashed back to the flames, the raging fires taking My Father from me. I thought of Valliance, how broken he was. I thought of my fathers' little used name Kallias, thinking of him like that seemed to be alien. Then I thought of Mother, I barely remembered the grief that faced me when I'd found out about her death. I vaguely recalled her burning. When I was young, they thought it best to veil me. I remember watching the fire through that black gauze and I remembered crying. But that was all. I scarcely remembered the events of the day. And now I question what my mother really meant to me, did I not feel this wild amount of loss and grief after her death, despite all the times we were together, despite all her lullabies, I felt little grief that day. After all I had handmaid's who could sing me those songs and tutors who could tell me her stories. Maybe I had no real personal connection with my mother like I did with my father. Now as I watched that empty battlefield with eyes stinging from holding back tears, I felt so fake and so empty. Maybe I'd never been strong. Maybe I did need my father to support me and I might have collapsed without him. Maybe I should not be queen.

Suddenly, I became aware of more presences behind me. I turned to see Leas, Tull, Deon and Asir all watching me. "What now my queen?" asked Deon with a bow, "What should be our next move to defeat these people?" I felt a warm glow inside me as I felt their confidence in me. I felt that they knew I should be queen, they were sure I'd do a great job of it and I felt my Father's confidence too. My stomach tingled as my mind formatted a plan, a dangerous, elaborate, crazy plan, but a plan no less and because I was queen of Charyass nobody could stop me. "We do just as my Father told us," I said decidedly, turning to face them with a grim and determined smile, "We find the ancient ones."

037

Printed in Great Britain
by Amazon